Triple Shot

Triple Shot

Sandra Balzo

W⊕RLDWIDE®

TORONTO • NEW YORK • LONDON
AMSTERDAM • PARIS • SYDNEY • HAMBURG
STOCKHOLM • ATHENS • TOKYO • MILAN
MADRID • WARSAW • BUDAPEST • AUCKLAND

Recycling programs
for this product may
not exist in your area.

Triple Shot

A Worldwide Mystery/February 2016

First published by Severn House Publishers Limited

ISBN-13: 978-0-373-26979-2

Triple Shot

Triple Shot

ONE

'GREAT HINDS MAY stink alike,' Sarah Kingston said, wrinkling her nose, 'but this one is particularly pungent.'

'Hey, don't look at me.' Art Jenada raised his hands, either in innocence or to ward off the foul odor that was permeating the Brookhills Wisconsin coffeehouse that Sarah and yours truly, Maggy Thorsen, operate.

'Just ignore her, Art,' I said from behind the counter. 'And, Sarah, before you insult the rest of our customers, I noticed the smell when I opened up this morning. Only now it's getting worse.'

Art was a neighbor, his catering business diagonally across the street from Uncommon Grounds. Our shop—now in its second incarnation—had opened just the month before in a historic train depot at the west end of a commuter rail line to Milwaukee. In fact, the service counter I now stood behind had been the station's original ticket windows. The building had been in Sarah's family for decades, the property eventually passing down to her.

Which was one of the reasons I put up with my always downright outspoken—and often outright rude—business partner.

That, and I've truly become fond of Sarah. Being

her friend is like having your own, evil alter-ego without the guilt.

My alter-ego's eyes were wide with innocence now. 'But I didn't accuse anybody, Maggy. Besides, a baby hippo feeding on rotted seaweed couldn't cut a fart of this magnitude.' Sarah fanned her face with an open palm. 'I just don't think Art's got it in him.'

Art looked like he wasn't sure whether to agree or disagree. But then, he wasn't given the chance to choose either.

'*Ohmigod!*'

We all turned to see Tien Romano coming out of the kitchen. She used a thumb and forefinger to pinch closed the nostrils of her pretty nose. 'The smell's become worse since I started baking.' Tien sounded like she was bearing up under a heavy head cold. 'I bet we have mice and some of them died in the wall.'

Great. Many of us connected to Uncommon Grounds had worn more than one hat in life, but none, to my knowledge, bore an exterminator logo on it. I had been in public relations and Sarah ran—though these days, kind of remotely—Kingston Realty.

Tien, along with her father, Luc, had owned a market and butcher shop. Now he was retired and she was our chef, responsible for the homemade pastries and soups, sandwiches and packaged meals we sold to commuters office-bound in the morning and homebound in the evening.

Tien pointed toward our street-side front entrance. 'Maybe we should open the door.'

As she said that, the sleigh bells attached to its top jingled. While the door was swinging fully open, the four women sitting in tennis togs at a nearby café table simultaneously hunched their shoulders and grabbed for their napkins.

A racquet-and-ball drill team? No, just seasoned Wisconsinites bracing for the winds of impending winter, following the cruel joke we refer to as 'Indian Summer'.

The prior five days, our October weather had been unseasonably mild, the thermometer hitting a high of seventy-nine degrees Fahrenheit yesterday. By Wednesday morning, though, the temp had plummeted to near-freezing and the tennis—along with any potted plants—had been moved indoors.

An unwelcome development for most of the population, but for a coffeehouse it was nirvana come to earth. Hot drinks were selling like...well, hot cakes. Especially the 'Triple Shot, fully-loaded' latte I had just made for Art. The autumn specialty drink had enough caffeine and sugar to warm the cockles of the coldest heart. And maybe even send it into fibrillation.

'Close the door,' the tennis quartet sang out.

The man who obeyed was fortyish and dapper. You'd never guess his arms were usually covered to the elbows in the blood of sea-creatures.

'Zee wind, she is a bitch out there,' Jacque Oui said. 'Oh, how I long for zee south of Fronce.'

Tien's face lit up at the sight of Brookhills' fishmonger to the stars and owner of Schultz's Market. 'Jacque, you are the only person I know who can make "bitch" sound sophisticated.'

I was a little surprised by the adoration in Tien's voice, though maybe I shouldn't have been. Tien looked at Jacque as intriguingly foreign though she, herself, was the true exotic flower. Italian-American on her father's side and Vietnamese on her mother's, Tien represented the best of all her worlds.

'The hell with "zee south of Fronce",' Sarah said, caricaturing Jacque's accent and sentiment. 'I'd take zee south of *Chicago* right now.'

Where the mercury was probably hovering in the balmy forties.

I sniffed. 'South of Chicago is Gary. Which, come to think of it, smells pretty close to—' I gestured widely and vaguely—'our establishment right now.'

The industrial city in northernmost Indiana had a reputation for its flame-belching, Mordor-like smokestacks and malodorous haze. A well-earned one, I thought, at least judging by the last time I'd driven through, my windows up and air vents set on 'RECIRCULATE'.

'Gary has its steel mills to blame,' Art said, sniffing, too. 'What's Uncommon Grounds' excuse?'

A little brutal, especially given my earlier defense of him. But like our county's sheriff Jake Pavlik, the love of my life—or at least of the second half of that span—Art was a native of greater Chicagoland. The caterer was just standing up for a sister-city, albeit one with an atmospheric ambience beyond dragon's breath.

'You're right, Art,' I said. 'We have no excuse here. Like Tien suggested, maybe opening the street-side door—and, I guess, the platform one—would cross-ventilate the place.'

Sarah snorted, then winced from the air she drew in. 'If our customers have to choose between asphyxiation and hypothermia, they'll vote with their feet and brave the outside world.'

'Sarah?' I said quietly.

'What?'

'You have a better plan?'

Her features twisted into an expression that reminded me of the old Cabbage Patch dolls. Which was answer enough for me. Not for the first time, I surveyed our layout.

The coffeehouse was square, with the service area, office and kitchen forming a smaller square snugged into the back right corner, thereby creating an 'L' of public space. The shorter base of that 'L' paralleled the street out front and was filled with café tables. The long leg was lined with a high bar-top and stools where customers could sit facing the windows that overlooked the train tracks. The bar-top ended at the doorway to the train's boarding platform. Across a corridor from that platform door were our restrooms.

As I pushed out the swinging gate that connected the serving area with the public part of the shop, our mail carrier, Ann, came through our street-side entrance. Ignoring the chorus of 'brrr's' in her wake, she nodded to me without breaking stride and dropped a rubber-banded stack of envelopes at a service window. Then Ann wheeled about-face on her heel and quick-marched back outside.

'Wow, Ann's in a hurry today,' I said, continuing toward the platform door.

'She was—wisely—holding her breath,' Sarah said, picking up the mail packet and fanning the air with it as she followed me. 'The only reason those Brookhills

Barbies are still here is that their own perfume is out-reeking the aforementioned baby hippo that died beneath our floorboards.'

'Shhhh.' I looked over my shoulder at the foursome in tennis skirts, a subset of the larger population of Brookhills Barbies.

As unnaturally proportioned and coiffed as the dolls of the same name, most of the women were also Barbie-plastic in their personalities. Plastic, though, being just one of the elements from the Brookhills Periodic Table that often included silicone and saline, collagen and Botox.

'Oh, come on, Sarah,' I said, pushing the platform door wide open and sucking in a lungful of chilly air, 'it's certainly not *that*…oh, dear Lord!' I put my hand to my mouth. Cross-ventilation would be less the stink-solution and more the vehicle for spreading the problem.

As I closed the door, Sarah was staring down at a fat envelope. 'What the hell?' She ripped the thing open.

I knew to keep my mouth shut. Not that hard now, since, despite being indoors, I was still trying not to breathe at all. Sarah seemed to absorb the gist of the document she'd unfolded.

Finally, my ever-circumspect partner looked up. 'That bitch is dead.'

TWO

THE WAY SARAH KINGSTON pronounced bitch didn't rhyme with 'beach' and, also unlike Jacque Oui's version, was about as far from 'sophisticated' as you could get.

'Who's dead?' I asked, though it probably should have been 'which', as in 'which bitch'. We certainly had enough of them to go around, and somebody usually felt justified in wanting to kill one of us.

Sarah shook the sheaf of papers like a tantrumming toddler would a rattle. 'Brigid Ferndale, who else?'

Brigid was new to Kingston Realty and, although I'd met the pretty young woman only once, she'd impressed me as smart and ambitious. In fact, I'd warned Sarah to watch out or Brigid would be outselling her in a year.

Maybe the rookie already had.

My partner was now flipping through pages, apparently skim-reading the dense paragraphs. 'I could kill the—'

'Shh,' I said, noticing that one of the tennis Barbies had nervously stuck her head around the corner. Slim to the point of emaciation, with hair so blonde and fine it was nearly colorless, she looked surprised to see us. Or maybe she'd had a recent browlift.

'Oh, dear. I'm so sorry.' Her voice, with just a trace

of Southern lilt to it, was barely audible. Raising her hand in evident apology, she retreated.

'Uh-oh,' I said, wondering how much the woman had heard. 'Isn't she a broker, too?'

'Holly Hobby,' Sarah snapped, without looking up at me.

'Pardon? I thought her name was Elaine Riordan.' In fact, I was almost certain. In addition to selling real estate, the woman headed the Brookhills County Historical Society and had tried to get me to do one of those fund-raisers where the police 'arrest' and lock you away until you call enough friends to raise 'bail', as in a contribution to the charity involved.

I'd finally convinced Riordan that my friends didn't like me that much.

'Maggy, don't be an idiot,' Sarah said, making my point. 'I know what her name is. And I assure you she's just another rich chick who thinks it's "fun" to show and sell houses. Only Elaine Riordan's an embarrassment even to her own breed.'

'Her "breed"?'

'Women like Gabriella Atherton and her new agency. Holly Hobbies, Broker Barbies. Call them what you will, but each one comes with stilettos, a designer briefcase, and a penchant for stealing money from *real* brokers like me.'

As a little girl, I'd never cared much for any of the 'career' Barbie Dolls. No Flight Attendant, Ballerina or even Surgeon Barbie on *my* childhood Christmas list. No, I wanted Malibu Barbie, with the sun-kissed skin and smoky, bedroom eyes. Hell, I wanted to *be* Malibu Barbie.

But alas, my bra-burning earth mother deemed the tanned lady a tramp. Not only was there no Malibu Barbie under the tree, but my stocking was filled with homemade granola, carob-covered raisins, packs of almonds and an apple.

Christmas-morning disappointments aside, though, I was pretty sure that Barbies—real or toy—weren't the cause of Sarah's temper tantrum. 'OK, I get it. You don't like dilettantes nibbling chunks of your profession's cheese. But what does any of this have to do with Brigid Ferndale and that?'

I pointed at the sheaf. As Sarah turned her wrist, I could see a State of Wisconsin insignia on its envelope.

She finally reached the last page, but then just turned back to the first. 'The little rat-bastard's reported me to the realty board.'

'For what?'

'My "apprentice" claims I've "failed to provide her the oversight and training required by regulations".'

'Have you?' To my knowledge, Sarah had barely set foot in Kingston Realty for at least the last few weeks. 'Failed, I mean?'

A shrug. 'Kind of, but that was Theodore's job as our "supervising" broker.'

'I thought you fired him. Like unto a month ago.'

'I had to. He was hitting on Brigid.'

Not a surprise. Theo knew houses, but was otherwise a sleazeball extraordinaire. 'Well then, how about…ach, what's her name? The one with the tats who looks like a professional wrestler?'

'Polly?'

Of course. I should have remembered because it

rhymes with Holly, as in Sarah's derisive 'Holly Hobby'. But this woman was no doll.

'She quit,' Sarah continued. 'Said the job was too dangerous.'

'What?' Polly sure looked like she could take care of herself. 'Selling real estate?'

'Didn't you hear about the agent who was shot through the head and left to die in a penthouse condo just last week? And another one yesterday, first a head-shot and then a tumble down a split-level colonial's flight of basement stairs.'

I had heard. In fact, my boy-toy Pavlik and his sheriff's department were working both cases. One of the reasons I hadn't seen much of him recently. 'I assumed they were independent incidents. Or, at worst, a local crazy.'

'I wish,' Sarah said. 'Across this great country of ours more than twenty agents were killed on the job last year. The National Association of Realtors has survey results on its website. A quarter of the respondents said they're now carrying guns to protect themselves while working.'

OK, upon reflection, meeting strangers at vacant homes or driving them around in my car weren't tasks I'd feel particularly comfortable performing. Though, for me, toting a gun would be atop that list. I'd probably shoot myself, saving my attacker the trouble.

No, I'd much prefer taking my chances with some of the self-defense moves Pavlik had taught me one particularly memorable evening.

I'd nearly had my purse stolen the day before, so Pavlik was giving me his 'be aware of your surroundings' lecture for the nth time, as I made us dinner at my place.

'What good does it do me to "be aware" of danger,' I'd said, turning toward him with a carving knife in my hand, 'if I can't protect myself from it?'

After he disarmed me, we decided that in lieu of dessert we'd retire to the bedroom for a game of strip 'don't-let-'em-poke-her'.

Pavlik would show me a self-defense tactic, and each time I executed it correctly, he'd take off a piece of his clothing.

I proved a fast learner.

'The sole of a flat shoe on your major foot, cocked at a forty-five degree angle to the attacker's knee cap, then driven downward, dislocating the joint.'

Not exactly romantically put, but...gotcha. Off with the shirt, mister.

'Elbow, or pinky edge of your hand, smashing the attacker's nose, followed by the heel of your palm thrust up into said broken beak.'

Okey-dokey. Down go those jeans.

'Maggy?'

'When choked from the front or behind, lifting your major leg—high heels now actually preferable—and stomping down with all your might on his instep, depressing and even fracturing the tiny, sub-surface bones in—'

'Maggy!'

I hadn't realized my eyes were closed. Sarah was giving me the Cabbage Patch expression again. 'Are you all right?'

'Sure. Just daydreaming.' And rudely awakened, I

might add, before I got to the nitty-gritty. Or tighty-whities, more accurately.

'God. Could you please stay in the context of a real world conversation?'

Probably not, but I'd give it a try.

The subject, I thought, had been armed real estate agents. 'You still have your pistol?' I asked Sarah, who had saved my life with one in the not-so-distant past.

'First of all, Maggy, I prefer revolvers. Pistols, also known as semi-automatics, have too many safeties. There's a risk the bullet won't fire when I pull the trigger.'

Risky safeties. Who was the oxymoron now? 'All right, then. Do you still have your *revolver*?'

'Yes and no. The one you remember was a Charter Arms Bulldog, but the hammer kept getting snagged on the key rings of the houses I was showing. Though I'm not sure why, that seemed to queer a couple of deals for me, so I switched to a Smith & Wesson Bodyguard because it has a shrouded hammer.'

'Shrouded?'

'Yeah, so it doesn't stick out from the frame. Then—wouldn't you know it?—I found I liked wearing a holster better anyway.' She smacked herself upside the head.

Wasn't that always the way? You buy carpeting to match the drapes and somebody burns down the house.

Sarah glanced first toward the front of the shop and then back toward the restrooms. 'Since we're alone, hold these.'

I took the sheaf of papers and watched her right hand slip under the long, baggy jacket she always wore over belted trousers. When the hand came back out it was holding a mean-looking pistol—sorry, revolver.

Lovely. The perfect accessory for any woman's wardrobe.

Sarah pointed the muzzle toward the floor and thumbed something on the side of her 'Bodyguard'. The cylinder part rolled out and to the left of the weapon's frame but still attached to it.

'What are you doing now?'

'Making sure it's loaded.'

Better and better. 'So, that little scored button on the top is the only part of the "hammer" that sticks out?'

'Right.' Sarah, again with the thumb, gently rolled the cylinder back into the frame and then wiggled it until I heard another click. 'Now a chamber is centered for the firing pin.'

Eyeing the gun warily, I said, 'This revolver looks bigger than your Bulldog. Is it?'

'A little, but the main advantage of this beauty is that it holds five big-ass, .357 magnum rounds.'

Holy shit. Even *I'd* heard of those. 'You carry a .357 magnum?'

'I don't *always* carry it, Maggy.'

Reassuring. 'But a .357 magnum,' I repeated. 'Like in *Dirty Harry*?'

'No, Clint Eastwood used a .44-caliber magnum, even more powerful still. C'mon, Maggy, what *do* you want me to protect myself with? A derringer? Or one of those puny .22-and .32-caliber Beretta Bobcats or Kel-Tecs? They're popular with a lot of real estate agents because they don't weigh much, but I ask you, what's the point of packing if a slug won't drop the bad guy in his tracks?'

I wasn't getting into this with her. 'So if Polly was worried about safety on the job, why didn't she just get a gun, too?'

'I told her it was a good idea. Even offered to pay for the gun-safety course.' Sarah sounded disgusted. 'But, no. *She* preferred to run away and marry her coked-up boyfriend.'

Ahh, yes. Polly wants a crack head. Now *that* should reduce her exposure to firearms.

I tried to summarize: 'OK, arsenal aside, let me get the personnel aspect straight. You fired your office's supervising broker fearing a sexual harassment claim against him, and Polly quit in fear of her life. Which means you've been leaving your young apprentice Brigid sitting there alone with no training and nothing to do?'

'Of course not. There's plenty to keep her busy. Showings, open houses. But *always*, with somebody as shotgun guard.'

'Sarah, you have no "*some*bodies" left, with or without shotguns.'

A dismissive wave. 'Figure of speech. Besides Brigid knows a lot of people. I mean, how many employers tell you to invite your friends over while you're working?'

Only ones desperately in need of additional staff.

'I'm a good boss.' Sarah back-pedalling. 'You said yourself how capable and eager Brigid is. So I gave her free rein, let her write the occasional offer-to-purchase and balance our clients' trust account. I was even going to let her do the Williams' open house on Sunday, though now MaryAnne wants it late Friday afternoon.'

MaryAnne Williams was one of the Barbies enjoying our coffee out-front, but unlike the woman who'd peeked around the corner, she hadn't homogenized her appearance to join the clique. In fact, MaryAnne was the high-resolution version of fading Elaine Riordan, right down to the Southern accent. Big and naturally blonde, ballsy and…well, imagine the volume punched up ten notches on Riordan's wispy lilt and you'd pretty much have MaryAnne's timbre. And she herself would tell you she didn't care 'a fig' about fitting in, here or anywhere else.

Still, I shook my head. 'An open house on Friday afternoon? Everybody's at work.'

'Apparently not the people who can afford that house. Besides, MaryAnne wants us to serve wine and cheese so people can stop by on their way home, even if they actually have a job.'

'Not a bad idea,' I said. 'A one-time happy hour, like those clothing boutiques sometimes—'

'I still can't believe that little ingrate is ratting me out to the state. Here, trade. Just keep the muzzle pointed down.' Sarah thrust the revolver at me and took back the papers. 'See, Maggy? Look at this.'

I held the gun gingerly with both hands and tried to read the line next to where her index finger was tapping. 'OK. Unlicensed real estate apprentices aren't supposed to do what you—'

'They're not supposed to do *any*thing, at least for the first six months. But what good is that to me? Or any other broker's business?'

'I think you might be missing the point of mentoring.'

'Yeah? Well, maybe Ms Brigid Ferndale is "missing the point" of being an apprentice.'

'Apprentice or indentured servant?'

'I've been paying her a perfectly fair salary, as detailed in—' Sarah flipped to another page— 'this.'

I looked at her second 'this'. It was a contract, evidently filed with Wisconsin's Department of Regulation and Licensing, in which Sarah promised to provide Brigid with a salary and also stipulated her hours, 'course of study' and a schedule of commissions she would be paid upon completion of the apprenticeship.

'Comprehensive,' I said. 'Right down to what you were *supposed* to be teaching her.'

'And then she goes behind my back and files a complaint? The Division of Enforcement is going to be on this like flies on horseshit. Who knows what irregularities an auditor might find, with me out of the office so much.'

Out of the office so much? That was putting it mildly and, besides, more argument for the prosecution than evidence for the defense. Sarah had essentially gone AWOL, preferring to sell coffee over property. And she'd left a kid in charge of her realty gig.

Even Brigid—eager as she might be to get ahead— knew that was a mistake.

Though I had to take some of the blame, too. Sarah had abdicated her office to become *my* business partner.

'I'm sure it'll be fine,' I said weakly as Sarah took back the gun.

'Try to sound like at least *you're* convinced of that,'

Sarah growled as she pushed aside her jacket and slipped the gun back into the holster attached to her belt.

Elaine Riordan hovered tentatively at the corner again. Apparently she'd left her tennis gear in the car, but slung over her shoulder was a strapped bag expansive enough to hold a frou-frou dog. And with enough buckles and hardware on the outside to convince any potential hairy Houdini not to make a break for it.

I cleared my throat. 'Can I help you?'

'I'm so sorry, but I need to use the restroom?' Her tennis soles squeaked as she did a pitiful little potty dance.

I tugged Sarah to one side and Riordan hurried past us at a dead run.

I'm not sure my partner even noticed. She was still staring at her sheaf of papers, muttering.

'Is there anything I can do?' I asked.

The bells on the street-side door jingled but Sarah didn't look up.

Nor did she answer me.

I sighed and had started back toward the front of our shop when a familiar voice stopped me. 'My God, what is that *stench*?'

I could retreat, but Sarah, still growling, wasn't much of an alternative. The proverbial rock and a hard place, but in this case, it was more caught between the bitchy and the bitchier.

Told you Brookhills is rife with them.

Kate McNamara, editor and publisher of the *Brookhills Observer* and occasional on-air reporter for our regional cable news operation, stood inside the door, literally holding her nose. Next to her was a tall, dark-

haired man gracefully graying at the temples, his camel
sports jacket unbuttoned, Burberry scarf arranged just-
so at his neck. Right behind him, as though she was
drafting in his wake, came an angular young blonde
wearing jeans and a parka. She didn't register with me,
but the man looked vaguely familiar.

Noticing the others also reacting to our air-quality
index, I said, 'Sewer problem.' To tweak the journalist,
I added, 'Surely someone called a breaking story like
this into your paper, Kate?'

Tien, her work done for the day, had departed, along
with Jacque. Art had taken his coffee to the bar-top
facing the window where he clacked away at his computer. Next to Elaine Riordan's empty chair, a streaked-
blonde Barbie sat texting, while MaryAnne and a fourth
woman, a rare brunette in our town, had their heads together looking at a newspaper.

All, apparently, was right with the world. At least,
Brookhills-style.

'Art, you need anything?' I asked as I circled behind him.

He shook his head without bothering to look up from
the screen, so I turned to the newcomers. 'Morning,
Kate. What can I get you?'

I wanted to find out who the man accompanying her
was, but I knew from previous experience with Kate
that any question beyond the one I'd already posed
would just result in an unadvancing litany of her new
conquest's credentials, both personal and professional.

However, as the Bible says: Don't asketh and it shall
be given unto you anyway. Or words to that effect.

'Maggy, surely you know who this is,' Kate practically purred.

'I'm afraid I haven't the faintest.'

'No? How about Chicago?'

Mercifully, before I could burst into a song from the musical, the man stepped up to me. 'Ward Chitown.'

He pronounced it 'shy-town'. I stuck out my hand. 'Maggy Thorsen.'

'You're kidding.' Sarah had come up behind us.

Chitown bypassed my hand and extended his to her. 'Ah, I see my reputation has preceded me.'

'Reputation?' Sarah shook hands, while managing to whisper—audibly—to me, 'I just thought it was a stupid name—Ward "Chitown" from "Chicago"?'

'Shit!' Art Jenada's head had swiveled around from his computer. 'Ward, is that really you?'

Chitown, once-burned by Sarah's attitude, was now twice...well, 'chi'. 'Umm, yes?'

Art hopped off his stool and, nudging past the young woman in the winter jacket, went to pump the other man's hand. 'Damned if it *isn't*. How've you been? What brings you up here to the boonies?'

'Chi-town' was a nickname for Chicago, though not as popular as 'The Windy City'. Or even 'Second City', though some of its residents might bristle at the implication that Chicago was Avis to New York's Hertz. Probably the same people who considered everything north of the Cubs' Wrigley Field the 'boonies'.

'Can I get you something, Kate?' I asked again.

And was roundly ignored. Again. 'You haven't read our *Brookhills Observer*,' Kate scolded Art. 'Or even seen the television news. Ward's producer here has been scouting our jewel of a town since last week and Ward arrived on Sunday. They're going to stage *The Treasure of the Brookhills Massacre* this Saturday.'

'*Stage?*' It was less a word and more an intake of air from the blonde, presumably the aforementioned, but as yet not introduced, producer.

Chitown glanced back at her. 'Deirdre is quite right, Katy.'

Uh-oh: I'd never heard anybody call Kate McNamara 'Katy' before. I bellied up to the service window to get a better view of the carnage.

But alas, Chitown continued unbloodied. 'We don't "stage" what is, quite simply, a search for the truth.'

'No, no, of course not,' Kate said, her face reddening to the point that the freckles marking it nearly disappeared into their background. 'I meant "stage" only in the logistical—'

But Art Jenada had fixated on his homeboy. 'Ward, I haven't seen you for ages. Really miss you, man. How're the wife and kids?'

With ten million people in the greater Chicago area, the chances of two people meeting there and subsequently stopping by my Brookhills coffeehouse had to be...'You really do know each other?'

'Well...' Chitown hedging. 'I don't believe I've had—'

But Art just talked over him. 'Ward here is legendary in Chicago. First, as an investigative reporter, and then being the host of *Chitown on Chi-Town*. That ran for—what—twenty years?'

'Twenty-two,' Chitown corrected.

'A TV show?' I guessed.

Art growled under his breath. 'Not *just* a TV show, Maggy. It was the number one, local noontime program in the country during its heyday.' Art turned back to Chitown. 'I don't expect you to remember, but you had me as a guest once.'

'I...?'

Art forgave him with a wave. 'Ah, of course you don't. There must've been hundreds of guests on that show over the years.'

'Thousands,' Chitown said, seeming to relax in the warm pool of adoration Art was ladling onto his feet. 'But you do look familiar, Mr...um...? Wait a second, the first name...it's Art, right?'

'Right!' Art turned to me, beaming. 'Amazing, isn't he? Like I said, a genuine legend.'

More like a genuine good listener. Just a few minutes ago, Chitown should have heard me ask 'Art' if he wanted a refill of his coffee.

But, then, in my experience good listeners are even rarer than legends. I gave our visitor a wide smile and the benefit of my doubt. 'Well, a hero to Art deserves a drink on the house. What can I get you and your producer?' I extended my hand to the woman. 'Is it Deirdre?'

'Yes, Deirdre Doty,' she said, shaking. And not just my hand. The slim woman was shivering even in the heavy coat, and her clasp was like ice.

'You poor thing, you're freezing.' I pointed to the dry-erase board that highlighted our specials. 'Our fall Triple Shot Latte should warm you up.'

'"Triple Shot, fully-loaded",' Doty read aloud. 'What's it loaded with?'

'Sugar,' Sarah said. 'A little fat on those bones would provide insulation. Or are you one of those fitness freaks?'

I ignored my business partner, hoping Deirdre Doty would do likewise. 'It's also good *un*sweetened or artificially sweetened, if you like.'

'No, I think the sugar would be nice, but maybe without the milk,' Doty said, glancing at Chitown. 'It would be like our Café Cubano, Ward. All over again.'

I'd had Café Cubano, or Cuban coffee, when visiting South Florida. It's strong, sweet and amazingly smooth—almost creamy. 'Exactly like one, Deirdre, only super-sized, in the American tradition. But I'm afraid I don't stock demerara sugar.'

Deirdre Doty seemed impressed I knew of the unrefined sugar, similar to turbinado, but coarser. 'Whatever you have is fine.'

'Some turbinado, then.' I put a couple of heaped spoonfuls of the natural sweetener in the bottom of a small cup and set it aside. Then I positioned the basket of our long-handled portafilter under the cone grinder and pulled the lever twice, releasing a measured amount of espresso before twisting the filter onto the espresso machine, placing a small stainless steel pitcher below it to catch the brew and pushing the button. 'Would you like one, too, Mr Chitown?'

'Ward, please. And I'd love it *con leche*, if you can.'

Literally, coffee with milk. Or, in this case, espresso with milk, which was what a latte was in the first place.

'Easily,' I said, reaching for a larger version of our stainless steel espresso pitcher. 'Whole milk?'

'Please, though I know it's decadent. Deirdre is made of sterner stuff and drinks the brew straight.'

'I'm afraid I don't have anything to use for jolts,' I said to Doty, knowing that Cuban establishments provide customers with a stack of thimble-sized plastic cups, so the caffeine and sugar-laden beverage could be divvied out and tossed back like Jell-O shots.

'In a cup is just fine,' she said, 'since we don't need to share like when we were on assignment in Miami. Remember, Ward?'

I could sense Kate McNamara, not a good 'sharer' herself, bristle at the idea of the other two off 'on assignment' together anywhere, but especially a hot and glamorous city like Miami.

And, more especially, sharing *any*thing.

'Deirdre is from Miami,' Chitown said, 'and showed us how a single, solitary Cuban coffee could fuel our whole crew.'

'Florida's Magic City,' I said, pouring Chitown's milk into the larger pitcher and sticking it under the frothing wand. Just managing to cut a look at Kate, too.

I'd nearly gotten the woman fired from her first television job and she'd nearly gotten me arrested for murder.

Made it tough to be friends. Not that I'd ever tried very hard.

I affected a sigh. 'Miami, so beautiful, so…romantic.' I poured a little espresso into Doty's cup to make a paste with the sugar.

'I'll have a large black coffee,' Kate snapped. 'And make these all to-go, before we pass out from the rat stench.'

Ahh, Kate. Insulting my shop by using 'stench' twice, but still trying to jump on the free-drink bandwagon. Well, let her twist in the wind.

Large black coffee: $1.75. Pissing off Kate McNamara? Priceless!

I slowly poured the rest of the espresso into the cup. The idea was to get foam when it mixed with the sugar paste.

'Bravo,' Chitown said.

'Thank you,' I said, gauging my work before I slid the cup across to Doty. 'I've never prepared it the traditional way before.'

'Nice,' said Sarah, approvingly. 'Usually Maggy just dumps all the crap in together.'

Not about to let my partner rain on my professional parade, I brewed—or 'pulled', as the technique is called—three more shots of espresso and followed the same ritual, this time in a full-sized coffee cup so I'd have room for the steamed milk. '*Voila.*'

'I said to-go,' Kate snapped again. A wonder she didn't crack a couple of teeth per day.

Art, who had been waiting patiently all this time for another opp with his hero, put an arm around Chitown and steered him to a table next to the Barbies. 'So, Ward, what brings you to our little town?'

'I told you,' Kate started irritably, as Deirdre Doty followed the men. 'He's—'

Sarah, having witnessed the entire exchange, whinnied like a plow horse. She has a long face and huge teeth, so she's disconcertingly good at it. 'Oh, Kate, let the man bask in adoration. He probably doesn't get much of it these days.'

I threw my partner a startled glance. 'You know this guy, too?'

Sarah shrugged. 'I get the Sunday *Chicago Trib*.'

I knew the *Tribune* was one of the big city's two daily newspapers. 'And it carried a feature about this Brookhills Massacre?'

'Of course not, idiot. A news story recounting Chi-town's ugly divorce. From his second wife. You know, a generation-skipping trophy one.'

I was thinking about the trip to Miami with Deirdre Doty and, supposedly, 'their' crew.

'Did his wife accuse him of cheating?' I asked, glancing over toward the table where Art, Chitown and Doty now sat, chatting.

'Nah, more like being a has-been.'

'Ward is no such thing,' Kate said indignantly.

Sarah held up her hands. 'Hey, scribe, give it a rest. I'm just quoting the man's wife.' Now back to me. 'Apparently he couldn't sustain the lifestyle to which she'd become accustomed.'

'So, she dumped him?'

'Hey, if a woman twenty years younger takes a shine to some guy, it's probably *not* because of his sparkling conversation.'

Sarah had a point. As my ex-husband Ted had found out when he dumped me for Rachel, *his* trophy wife, now once-removed. Permanently.

I'd opened my mouth to ask something further, but a hushed voice interrupted, 'Y'all want to know what *really* happened?'

THREE

'WE ALL' SWIVELED to see Elaine Riordan, our anorexic Southern belle, who'd finally returned from the restroom.

'What really happened where?' I asked, trying to look interested. It was a façade I mounted for our newer customers. The old ones knew me better.

Still, the details of Ward Chitown's marital breakup might prove more fascinating coffeehouse conversation than most.

But, alas, that didn't appear to be what Elaine Riordan had in mind. 'Why, at the Brookhills Massacre, of course.' Riordan moved closer, her big handbag slipping off a thin shoulder. She hitched it back up, sneaking an adoring glance at the table where the TV man and his flock sat. 'It's why Mr Chitown over there is in town and I'm happy to say the society has been able to provide his producer all sorts of information.'

'Your historical society?' I asked.

'Oh, yes.' Now Riordan was nodding like a bobblehead. 'News stories and the most awful photos. Even police reports.'

OK, my turn. 'I don't mean to sound stupid, but…'

'Too late.' Kate pulled a coffee cup toward her, then reached across the counter for a carafe and poured her own.

'…exactly what *is* the Brookhills Massacre?'

'It was a shoot-out, between the FBI and the Mafia?' Riordan said. 'A fascinating tale, especially for Mr Chi-town, whose own father was the special agent-in-charge that day.'

'When was all this?' I asked again.

'1974,' Riordan said. 'And it took place right across the tracks from you.'

I glanced out the train-side window. 'The old slaughterhouse?'

As I understood it, the building that faced us from over there had been used in the veal industry. Logical, of course, with the trains right there to bring in the cattle and ship out the meat, but just looking at the place gave me the creeps.

'No, Maggy. This happened just next door?' Riordan's Southern lilt made even simple declarative sentences sound like questions. 'At Romano's Ristorante.'

Romano's. As in Tien and Luc? Before I could ask my question of Elaine Riordan, Sarah diverted me with one of her own.

'A restaurant that's slaughterhouse-adjacent? Talk about your fresh meat. I mean, do you suppose it was like those seafood places that have lobster tanks in their dining rooms?'

'Meaning you finger Bessie out in the corral and they take her around back?' I asked.

Sarah nodded. 'Next time you see her, she's medium rare.'

Elaine Riordan looked genuinely horrified. Welcome to my world.

'Anyway,' Kate took up the story. 'Mobsters from all

around the Midwest were meeting in the restaurant's back room, divvying up cash skimmed from their Las Vegas casinos and sports books. In fact, Ward's father...' She called over to the man at the table. 'Ward, what was your father's name?'

Chitown, with an apology to Art, rejoined us. 'His name? Samuel.'

'No, no. His *last* name.'

'Why, Chitown, naturally. After all, I am his son.'

Sarah, as is her wont, put into words what we were all thinking. 'C'mon, man. You want us to believe that's on your birth certificate?'

'Of course it is.' Chitown looked offended. 'Probably pronounced differently when my ancestors arrived here, but as spelled out it most certainly was—and remains—our surname.'

Sarah still looked skeptical, but I said, 'Was your father killed in the raid?'

Chitown shook his head. 'No, thank God. He lived to retire from the agency and died just this past year, in fact.'

Riordan stuck her hand out to Chitown. 'I'm sorry for your loss, sir, but it's truly an honor to meet you. I'm Elaine Riordan, of the County Historical Society?'

'Oh, yes, Ms Riordan. I appreciate the help you've given Deirdre on my behalf.'

Everything, seemingly, revolved around Ward the Sun.

And Elaine Riordan certainly wasn't immune to his gravitational pull. She hadn't let go of the man's hand. 'Were you able to obtain access to the buildings? I believe there's split ownership, with the slaughterhouse

having reverted to the county? But as I told your producer, I'd be more than happy—'

'Oh, yes. Yes,' Chitown said, gently extricating his
hand from her grip. 'We'll be all set. And, again, thank
you so much.'

'Don't look now—' Kate said, nodding toward the
table where Riordan had been sitting—'but your friends
are leaving.'

MaryAnne Williams was nowhere in sight when
I turned, the brunette was scuttling out the door and
the drag Barbie—in relative position, not manner of
dress—was gathering her handbag.

Riordan ignored Kate and returned to bobble-head
mode. 'In fact, six men died that day. Three were La
Cosa Nostra lieutenants and the others FBI agents?'

Chitown mimicked her nodding. 'With two men
wounded, my father included.'

'Only one man left standing,' Riordan intoned sol-
emnly. 'Or running, should I say?'

Chitown looked at her appreciatively. 'You really do
know this story.'

'I find all history fascinating, but this case, what with
the mob connection and the missing…loot?'

'Loot?' I asked.

'Until now, the *consigliere* was thought to have escaped with the money,' Chitown explained.

OK, I admit when I'm lost. Or more lost. '*Consigliere?*'

'The "counsel" for Chicago's "Outfit", the orga-
nization that demanded tribute be paid by the local
Milwaukee family. The big-city *consigliere*—an at-

torney—attended the meeting to keep peace between the different factions.'

Keeping the peace, I thought. Like a marshal in the old west, but in this case the 'good' town-folk were a bunch of squabbling mobsters.

'I believe you just said "until now"?' If Elaine Riordan's eyebrows went any higher she'd have to pluck her hairline. 'Have you uncovered new information, Ward? Is that the reason you've reopened the case?'

I registered Riordan's switching to 'Ward', but it was her last two words I repeated to the man. 'The case? Are you here in some sort of law enforcement role?'

Chitown didn't look the part, but then neither did Jake Pavlik when he was riding his Harley, me as passenger behind him, my arms wrapped around his buttery leather jacket.

'No, no. Merely an investigative journalist,' Chitown replied. 'But Elaine—if I may?—is correct. Some information has come my way that indicates that while the *consigliere* may have escaped, he did so with*out* the money.'

'But then where is it?' Riordan asked.

'That, my dear,' Chitown touched her nose with his finger, 'you'll need to tune in to see.'

Hmmm. First, Ward and Elaine and now the playful tap.

Riordan was blushing. 'But mightn't you need me before that? For local fact-checking, I mean?'

'Well, I'm not certain.' Chitown turned and raised his voice. 'Deirdre? What do you think? Can we use Elaine as a consultant?'

The producer joined us, looking annoyed yet resigned. I had a feeling she'd fielded this kind of request before. 'I suppose we could use an extra body.' Now to Riordan. 'Though I have to tell you, it's not going to be glamorous. You'd be less consultant, and more gofer.'

Riordan looked thrilled at the prospect of becoming 'an extra body', lackey-level or not. But before she could answer, Art Jenada, close personal friend that he was, walked over and clapped Chitown on the shoulder. 'Gotta go, but hope to see you around, Ward.'

'Oh, same. Definitely.'

Art, computer under his arm, headed around the corner toward the platform door or maybe the restroom. Our neighbor's prostate had been giving him fits lately and he seemed to spend more time in the men's room than the shop itself. Just the week before, I'd nearly locked Art in at closing-time, thinking he'd gone when he'd merely been going. And going and going.

Deirdre Doty set her empty cup on the counter. 'That was wonderful, Ms Thorsen. And it did warm me right up.'

The parka she was still wearing inside the seventy-two degree store might have had something to do with it, too.

Deirdre Doty might not be a fashionista, but I liked her. Chitown talked a good game, but I sensed it was this woman who got things done.

'Please, call me Maggy,' I said, clearing her cup. 'And it was a pleasure.'

'Same here. Ward—' she turned to her boss—'I need to make some calls and it will be easier from the hotel. If I take the car, can you get a lift?'

Both Kate McNamara and Elaine Riordan lit up like incoming runways at a rural airport.

'That's not a problem,' Kate started.

'I'd be more than happy to drive you,' Riordan said, then hesitated. 'We'd just have to walk to my car at the Historical Society. Or maybe I could go get it and—'

'Well, good then,' Doty said and took her leave, jingling out our front door.

The platform door opened simultaneously, probably Art Jenada finally leaving. But, as a result, cold air again roared through the temporary wind tunnel.

Bringing with it an unfiltered version of our atmospheric enemy.

The now undeniable smell of decaying flesh.

FOUR

'MAYBE IT'S THE missing concierge,' Sarah muttered as we trailed Ward Chitown, Kate McNamara and Elaine Riordan out onto the platform to investigate.

At Chitown's suggestion.

'*Consigliere*,' I corrected. 'And thirty-seven-year-old bodies don't smell much.'

'You'd be surprised. I dated this one guy when I was twenty-seven. He didn't believe in showering and—'

I held up my hand. Amazingly, for once, it silenced her. 'Smells to me like this godawful odor is coming from beneath our feet. Sarah, how do we get under the depot? Maybe a crawlspace?'

I assumed there wasn't a full basement or cellar under the depot because I'd never seen an interior depot door that could lead to one. Which, in itself, was fairly unusual in Wisconsin. The snow and ice, freeze and thaw of bitter winter weather required building footings to be safely below the frost line—four feet in our part of the state. Once at that depth, you might as well dig another yard or so and have a basement for protection against our other deadly weather fiend, the tornado.

Sarah and I were still standing on the loading platform. The other three had taken a right and gone down steps that led to a sidewalk and eventually to the parking lot behind our depot.

Immediately in front of us were train tracks and, to our left, the platform morphed into a quaint, railed porch that wrapped around the building, street side.

In spring and summer, patrons would be seated outside here enjoying our food and drinks. Now, though, the tables and chairs were interlinkingly chained by twisted steel cable, like we were afraid they'd escape. Or, more likely on a day like this one, be blown miles away.

I shivered as a gust of wind out of the north scoured my face. The good news was that my face included my nose, and the fresh air alleviated the smell for a moment. 'Well?'

'Well what?' Sarah had left the document from the state regulators in the store, but it obviously was still on her mind.

'*How* do we get under this thing?'

'*How* should I know?'

Cute. 'Because your father and aunt owned this place.' I was gritting my teeth both against the cold and to remain civil in the face of…well, Sarah. 'Like, maybe you played here when you were little?'

'They never wanted me around,' she said. 'For obvious reasons.'

I couldn't resist. 'Because they knew you were going to grow up into a haphazardly medicated, bipolar coffeehouse owner…'

Sarah's eyes shot me daggers.

'…with a heart of gold?' I added hastily.

'No.' Her voice dropped into 'measured' mode, as though she was talking to someone with an IQ of 60. 'Because of the criminals who tended to gather underfoot.'

I sighed. 'OK, I've had enough of the guessing games. Give.'

Sarah flopped a hand out, palm up, now in a mime's 'well, what did you expect' gesture. 'You know, the Family. They had their own waiting room.'

I'd heard of odder quirks, especially since her prior generation did own the place. But still... 'The family? Your family had a private waiting room?'

'Not my family, you idiot. *The* Family. As in the Milwaukee La Cosa Nostra—the topic of conversation, if I recall, just now back in the shop. How obtuse can you be?'

Pretty obtuse, apparently. Not to mention having the retention span of a disoriented hamster. 'Sorry. Let's start over. Are you saying this place was mobbed up?'

'No,' Sarah replied with a sniff. 'The Milwaukee Crime Family just had a private waiting room. So as not to be...bothered.'

'By who? Autograph seekers?'

'My father and aunt let the city's LCN build a room under the loading platform. To give their guys privacy.'

Not to mention mildew.

'Like I said,' Sarah continued as she led the way down the steps to the sidewalk, 'I wasn't allowed around here when I was a kid. I'm just telling you what I heard.'

'Which was?'

A resigned sigh. 'That the Mafioso would come to this waiting room by way of some secret passage under the tracks. They'd hear their train announced over the depot's public address system, then climb up and hop on, with nobody knowing the difference.'

'But wouldn't the conductor notice?' Amtrak-to-Chicago always managed to find *me* when I didn't have a ticket.

Sarah rolled her eyes. 'Please, Maggy. Do you honestly picture some ticket-taker blowing the whistle on the mob? He'd be dead before the club-car opened.'

'What about your family, though?' Realizing I'd seen no sign of Kate and the other two, I went to peek around the corner of the building to the parking lot. Nobody. 'You just said Daddy and Auntie knew.'

Sarah had followed me. 'I think what you know and what you admit—even to yourself—can be two entirely different things.'

Startled by the brief ray of introspection, I asked, 'Are you talking about your father and his sister?'

But now Sarah was staring past me and back toward the depot, a faraway look in her eyes. 'They found it.'

'The cash?' I whispered.

Sarah seemed to refocus. 'What cash?'

'You know, the loot. The booty, the filthy lucre?' I said. 'The gangsters were divvying up skimmed casino money when the FBI—'

'Not the feds, you idiot.' Sarah's hand pecked the air behind me like a chicken eating grain on the ground. '*Them*. Somebody must have found the entrance.'

I turned to see Ward Chitown and Kate McNamara waving energetically at us from under the stairs we'd descended.

'Ladies?' Chitown said, pointing as we approached. 'Behold.'

The floor of the loading platform was supported by a concrete block wall about four feet high. A wooden trellis covered with a thick, woody vine masked the blocks. The plant's leaves were dropping, but Sarah had promised me that next summer it would be covered in exotic, orange flowers.

'I don't see...' I shaded my eyes. 'Oh, are you talking about the trellis behind the steps? It's been partially pulled away.'

'That's exactly what I'm talking about,' Chitown said. 'Good eye, Maggy.'

Sarah actually harrumphed. 'Maggy *should* know what the thing looked like. I had to stop her from destroying the trumpet creeper.'

'It seemed dead,' I protested. 'Or next thing to.'

Sarah glared at me. 'Doesn't mean the creeper won't spring back to life.'

That hadn't been my experience with dead things, but I let it ride. 'I don't remember seeing a door of any type behind the trellis.'

'An actual *door*?' Chitown asked. 'I was just looking for any break in the wall. So that you could shimmy under the deck and see what might have died.'

I noted that he had no intention of 'shimmying' under there himself. All 'investigate' and no 'initiate'. Figured.

I shivered again, but not from the north wind. 'According to Sarah, there's a room under here that the mob used,' I said. 'Sort of a gangster-only departure lounge.'

'Really,' Chitown said, looking intrigued. 'I've never—'

'Oh, yes,' Elaine Riordan chimed in. 'That way they could slip into and out of the area, without being seen? There's even rumor of a connecting tunnel under the tracks. The existence of the room itself is quite well-documented in the papers we hold at the Historical Society. Though, until y'all arrived, I swear I was the only one who took any interest at all.'

The woman seemed pleased as punch to provide new information to the big man. Like my Old English sheepdog Frank, dropping a slobber-covered tennis ball in front of me to throw.

'An escape route,' Chitown said, and you could see the wheels in his sensationalistic mind begin to turn. 'From the Ristorante?'

'Presumably,' Riordan said. 'Which means who knows what we might find in the waiting room?'

I thought, 'we'? Gofer or not, Elaine Riordan had decided she wasn't just a fount of Brookhills trivia auditioning for an assignment, but rather already a part of Chitown's production crew.

'"The waiting room",' he echoed, as if picturing the words written in capital letters on a television screen. THE WAITING ROOM.

'Perhaps the loot?' Riordan said breathlessly, if a bit behind the curve of the conversation as I envisioned it.

Kate, who had been abnormally quiet so far—probably salting away information for a story in her weekly rag—glanced at Sarah and me before saying. 'Oh, no. Surely not.'

If I'd been able to detect Chitown's 'wheels-turning', I sure as hell could sense Kate's mental abacus click-clacking as she tried to calculate the magnitude of Sarah's 'cut' should the money be found on her property.

Or maybe, more important now, to calculate the chances of Sarah allowing Chitown's cameras into— cue dramatic music—the waiting room.

'Kate is right,' Chitown said. 'Let's not get ahead of

ourselves. First we need to go in and see what is causing this horrible odor.'

Oh, *now* he was willing to do the dirty work?

'Go in? How?' I asked, moving closer. 'As I said before, I've never seen a door back there. Sarah, have you?'

My partner shook her head.

'Maybe it's been walled up.' Riordan peered around us. 'You know, like in *The Cask of Amontillado*?'

'The what?' Sarah asked.

'*The Cask of Amontillado*. It's a wonderfully creepy tale, if you haven't read it. In fact, I may just have a copy of *The Best Short Stories of Edgar Allan Poe* with me.' She began digging through her huge doggy-bag. 'Somewhere.'

And emerged with an afghan.

No, not a bred-down version of the hound. This was the kind of afghan my grandmother had crocheted, right down to the variegated earth-toned yarn, zigzag pattern and lingering scent of fabric softener from the clothes dryer.

Except that Riordan's throw-blanket had a ball of yarn stuck to it.

'Oh dear.' Her face reddened as the woman tried to stuff the whole mess back into the bag.

Hey, it could be worse, I wanted to tell her. Apparently Sarah'd had firearms popping out of *her* bag, before she'd wisely gone to the handy holster.

Chitown seemed to take it all in before clearing his throat. 'Well, I doubt there was malicious intent, as with Poe's Montresor and the, uh, *un*fortunate Fortunato. But the fact is, especially given the passage of time, any door *could* have been sealed, so you may very well be right, Elaine.'

'And yet, so very wrong,' Sarah said, turning away from the scene to whisper in my ear. 'No wonder she's the butt of jokes among the Holly Hobbies. I'm embarrassed to be seen with Elaine here, and I don't have to work with her.'

When I first met Sarah Kingston, her mode of dress had been trousers and baggy jackets, the only requisite being the jacket have pockets generous enough to hold her cigarettes and lighter. My partner had given up the smokes, but not the uniform they accessorized. Meaning there wasn't a lot that embarrassed her.

But I was in Sarah's corner on this one.

The afghan was three-quarters contained when the ball of yarn made a run for it, hitting the ground and unraveling until its core disappeared under a shrub.

As Riordan dove after her dwindling resource, I examined the trellis. 'I could be wrong, but I don't remember this being pulled away when I looked at the vine.'

'Looked?' Sarah repeated. 'You don't "look" with an axe.'

'You *kill* with an axe,' from the prophet of doom under the bush. 'As in, "the brave knight cleaved the villain from helm to nave".'

Or helmet to navel, and presumably a quote from something else she'd read. Riordan needed to diversify beyond history.

Kate McNamara came up behind me. 'That's a trumpet creeper?' Evidently our intrepid correspondent also had a little trouble continuing in the context of a conversation. 'My parents had one in their Florida yard. It nearly took over the place.'

'See?' I said to Sarah. 'It's a noxious plant. I told you I should have cut it down.'

'That'd only make things worse,' Kate said. 'The monster is like a hydra. Every time you lop off an arm it grows ten more.'

'Actually,' Chitown interjected, 'according to Greek mythology, the serpent Hydra had multiple heads, not arms. And when one was lopped off, it grew two more, not ten.'

Yet another show-off.

Kate colored up. 'I'm just repeating what my father told me.'

'I'm sorry, Katy.' Chitown put a hand on her shoulder. 'I didn't mean to offend you *or* your father. I'm just a fan—embarrassingly close to the word's derivation, fanatic—of all things mythical.'

'Probably because he thinks he's God.' Sarah, again in my ear: 'And *not* small "g".'

Chitown was smiling at Kate. 'Sometimes I get carried away.'

'Katy' twisted her head to smile back.

Weird to see the journalist, always sure of herself to the point of nausea—mine, never hers—defer to Chitown.

I pulled at the top of the trellis and the lattice toppled away from the wall. I caught a cut portion of the vine just in time to keep it from hitting Kate in the face.

'Watch that,' she said, jumping back. 'The bastard's sap could give me a rash. Or...' A glance toward Chitown and Kate's color rose again, 'so I'm told.'

The picture of a woman in lust. Whether it was for the man or for his connections in a much bigger media market remained to be seen.

Nonetheless, Kate safely out of the way, I let the trellis go so it could fall harmlessly to the ground and wiped my hand on my jeans.

'Huh,' Sarah said. 'There really is a door.'

Sure enough, the severed section of vine interweaving with lattice revealed a wooden panel that had been hidden from sight by the stairs as well. The entrance was less than four feet high and tucked in a shadowy corner where the loading platform wall formed a right-angle with the foundation one of the depot itself.

Chitown turned first to me and then to Sarah, his eyes aglow with excitement, as though we were his parents and he knew the gift he'd pestered us for lay, unopened, before him.

I looked at Sarah. 'Somebody has to go in there. Might as well be him. Without a TV crew.'

Chitown nodded eagerly.

Kate stood behind his right shoulder and Elaine Riordan, yarn safely recovered and afghan stowed, his left. Media Man and his posse.

Such as they were.

Sarah, owner of the building, shrugged. 'Go for it.'

Chitown reached for the small doorknob and pulled.

Nothing happened.

'Maybe the thing wasn't installed according to code,' I said, referring to building regulations that required doors to open out so people inside couldn't be trapped against them during a fire.

I pushed against the door and it swung in.

Immediately, the smell and stale warmth hit us like we'd cross-ventilated a blast furnace.

'Oh, God.' Kate put both hands to her nose and mouth.

Although the door was swung wide, none of us had moved forward.

'Don't suppose you have a flashlight,' Chitown said.

'In the office,' Sarah said. 'Go get it, Maggy.'

'I'm not going to go get it.' God help me, I didn't want to miss anything. Hadn't I learned anything from history? Mine, I mean. 'You get it.'

'I'm not going to get it.'

'Maybe you should both—' Chitown started.

'Oh, for God's sake,' Kate McNamara said, reaching in with one hand to feel around on the wall left of the door. 'Anybody think of checking for a light switch?'

I heard a 'click', and an overhead bulb came on.

'It's wired for power?' I asked.

'For God's sake, Maggy,' Sarah said, 'it was the 1970s not the 1790s. We did have electricity way back then.'

'True, but…it's a secret chamber.' In my book, secret chambers do *not* have functioning lights.

Elaine Riordan tried to squeeze her nose in to peer around.

'Hey,' Sarah said, nudging her out of the way. 'My hidden room, not yours.'

'Yeah,' I said, moving Riordan one more place back in the pecking order. So far as I was concerned, when Chitown couldn't open the door, he'd lost his chance to enter first. Especially now that we could see where we were going.

Bumping into the man himself, Riordan deferred

and took her rightful position at the back of the line. Or nearly the back—Kate, looking pale, had moved to a grassy patch, where she bent over at the waist and hurled the undigested parts of her breakfast.

'Journalistic distance?' I asked.

She managed to nod, but then her hand went to her mouth and stayed there.

'Don't you ladies want me to go in before you do?' Chitown asked. 'I know it smells awful and—'

'Nah, I'm good.' Sarah hunched down to get through the low doorway, made scuffling noises and despite the new lighting, promptly disappeared.

'Are you OK?' I called, scuttling in after her and nearly breaking my own neck as I tumbled to join her on the floor.

'Watch out, there's a step down,' she said. 'Or two.'

'Fine time to tell me.' I stood first and gave Sarah my hand to help pull herself up. 'I guess we should have known by the size of the doorway and the height of the platform—' I pointed to the ceiling above us— 'that they would have had to dig deep to create a room where you could stand.'

Chitown's head appeared in the doorway.

'Step down!' Sarah and I chorused.

'Yes, thank you.' Chitown managed the stairs quite well, damn him. He was the type of man you had trouble imagining disheveled, much less crumpled into a pile of limbs on the linoleum.

I looked around. Serviceable, and even comfortable in a seventies' kind of way. Chairs and a leather—no, make that fake leather—couch on one side and a table and six chairs on the other, metal legs showing patches of rust. An avocado-tone refrigerator was up against the station-side wall and when I levered open the heavy door, even the appliance light came on.

Beer. Three bottles of Miller High Life and one of Pabst Blue Ribbon. Two cans of Schlitz and an Old Milwaukee.

'Ah,' Chitown said, snagging a Miller. 'The Champagne of Bottled Beer. And still cold enough to make your teeth jump.'

'Well,' said Sarah, 'at least some explanation for my sky-high electric bill.'

'The Milwaukee mob certainly supported their hometown breweries,' I observed.

A camera flash made us all reflexively turn. Sarah and me, the way we go through life—mouths open and eyes closed—but Chitown beaming the practiced smile of a celebrity.

He even held up his beer so you could read the label.

Product placement, however coincidental. 'You're good.' All those years in marketing had taught me to recognize a natural showman. PT Barnum had nothing on Ward Chitown. This man lived to be loved.

'Good, schmood. Put that thing away,' Sarah said to Elaine Riordan, who was madly pushing buttons on her cellphone, presumably to retrieve and examine the digital photo she'd just shot.

'I'm so sorry.' Riordan barely glanced up from her miniature screen. 'I was just documenting.'

'When you're in my building, you document nothing.' Sarah, growling, slammed the refrigerator door. 'Maggy, can you imagine how much this dinosaur has cost us just to keep that beer cold all these years?'

She and I both knew we were all ignoring the elephant in the room. The dead, stinky elephant.

I looked around as Sarah went to a closet door ajar on the far side of the room. The track lighting that ran down the center of the ceiling cast deep shadows both behind and beneath the furniture.

'Think a squirrel or field mouse died under the couch?' I said, a triumph of hope over experience as I kneeled down, trying to see into the dark.

'Maggy...' Chitown hesitated and started again. 'I hate to say it, but as a reporter I've been around quite a few dead creatures. This one smells...bigger. Much bigger.'

'Bigger?' I straightened up. I'd stumbled over corpses myself. Didn't mean that 'denial' wasn't my knee-jerk reaction. 'Like a rat?'

'Yeah.'

That last voice was Sarah's. She had swung open the door of the closet. Beyond her, accented by light from a mesh-covered vent in the ceiling, was an avocado-green toilet.

A bathroom. And Sarah's face matched the color of the outdated porcelain.

'So, it's just a rat?' What does it say about your life when you're relieved the dead smell in the secret Mafia hideaway beneath your only source of income is 'just' a rat?

'No.' It was hard to tell in the dim light, but Sarah's skin tone seemed to be getting closer to forest green.

I crossed the room to her, the stench registering stronger with each step. 'Sarah?'

Sarah stood stock-still, eyes closed.

I repeated her name.

My partner's eyes blinked open, the tears yielding to gravity as they trickled down her cheeks. 'I didn't mean it,' she whispered.

She was scaring me. This reaction wasn't Sarah-like. 'You didn't mean what?' I whispered back.

'That she was... Oh, God. I am so, so sorry.'

My friend shuffled aside and I saw the shadowy body on the floor.

A rat, all right. Only not of the rodent variety.

Brigid Ferndale, Sarah's tattletale sales apprentice from Kingston Realty.

FIVE

HER OPEN MATTE-FINISH EYES. The sewer-odor from the involuntary release of bladder and bowel soaking her short silver dress, overwhelmed by the putrefying stench of evolving decomposition, fueled by our unseasonable warm snap.

I had seen—and smelled—it all before.

'Is everything OK in there?' I heard Kate McNamara call from outside.

Sarah and I looked at each other.

'Close quarters, Kate,' I said. 'Why don't you stay where you are.'

As I reached the last word, I was nudging Chitown back before he could see what we had. Then I closed the bathroom door. Brigid deserved what little dignity some tardy privacy could give her and, honestly, Sarah had enough problems without an investigative reporter being third witness on the scene.

My partner collapsed onto the couch, staring. Her catatonic state reminded me uncomfortably of another partner, on another day, after finding another body.

'Could you wait outside, please?' I said to Chitown softly.

'I…um…' He looked back and forth between Sarah and the bathroom door, seemingly torn between not wanting to increase my partner's suffering and his journalistic instinct to know what caused it.

'Of course,' Ward Chitown said finally, chivalry overcoming curiosity. He put a hand on my shoulder. 'Would you like me to call 9-1-1?'

'No, thanks. I have kind of a direct line.'

BROOKHILLS COUNTY SHERIFF Jake Pavlik ducked his head through the doorway and saw Sarah and me, now both sitting on the couch.

I'd asked Ward Chitown to take Elaine Riordan outside, update Kate, and then wait with them to direct the emergency responders.

Logical, but my reason for getting rid of the audience was more personal.

'Sarah, are you all right?' I'd asked when we were alone.

She didn't answer, just patted her pockets, absently checking for a cigarette.

'You gave up smoking,' I reminded her, though I knew Sarah still struggled. It was like being an alcoholic—you could stop drinking, but that didn't mean you weren't an alcoholic. The urges were still there.

And, honestly, if I'd had a cigarette I'd have given it to Sarah. A drink wouldn't have hurt, either.

'She was my responsibility.'

I shifted on the couch to face my partner. 'You mean Brigid?' I asked gently.

'No. Mother Hubbard,' she snapped. 'How do you like her shoe?' Sarah waved her arms at our surroundings, back to her old self. For what that was worth.

Of course it was the Old Woman Who Lived in a

Shoe, not Mother Hubbard, but when Sarah was in these moods it was best to take the high road. The other ones led straight to hell.

'Brigid *was* your responsibility,' I said, holding up my hand to stop Sarah's objection to being quoted against herself. 'At work, you may have failed her.'

'I did not—'

Geez, even agreeing with Sarah couldn't shut her up. 'But unless Brigid was holding an open house in the bathroom of—' I made finger quotes—'the "waiting room", this had nothing to do with selling real estate.'

'What was she doing here, Maggy? How could—'

Pavlik stuck his dark, shaggy-haired head through the entranceway. 'Where?'

I pointed to the bathroom door. When you're as close as the sheriff and I were, who needed words? We could practically read each other's minds.

Pavlik's was thinking: *How the hell did I get myself involved with this broad? It's like I'm Lassie, she's Timmy, and every day is a new well.*

A sheriff's deputy had followed Pavlik in and the two of them crossed to the bathroom, the uniform opening the door.

'Jesus,' he said, clapping a hand over his nose.

Pavlik just continued in, the deputy reluctantly following.

When they emerged, the deputy quickstepped to the waiting room's entrance and left us. I heard him call to someone.

As Pavlik closed in on us, a man I recognized as a crime-scene technician entered. He nodded to Pavlik, but hesitated when he saw Sarah and me.

I shrugged.

An answering shrug and the two men moved back into the bathroom.

'Going to do his job,' Sarah said.

I looked at her. 'Please tell me you're not making potty jokes at a moment like this.'

'What?' She genuinely seemed puzzled.

'Never mind,' I said.

Pavlik returned again, probably for a while, since he sat in a chair across from us. 'Can you identify the deceased?' he asked, hooking a notepad from an inside pocket of his charcoal-gray topcoat.

Not the soft leather jacket he wore when riding his Harley, but the coat did look great on him, its color setting off his eyes, which could range from clear blue when he was laughing through gray to nearly black, when he was angry.

I'd seen them black and I have to admit it frightened me.

But maybe that was part of his fascination. Or, more accurately, my fascination with him.

That and the dark hair that curled at the nape of his neck. The feel of his hands on me. The mouth, when…

'Maggy?' The mouth spoke.

'I'm sorry,' I said, gathering myself. 'You asked if we know the—'

'Brigid,' Sarah, silent until now, said. 'Brigid Ferndale. She worked for me.'

'For you?' Pavlik glanced between us. 'In the coffeehouse?'

I shook my head.

'Shit.' Pavlik rubbed his temple. 'You're saying the deceased was a real estate agent?'

'Apprentice,' Sarah said. 'In my office.'

'Kingston Realty, correct?'

'Correct.'

Pavlik scribbled on his pad. 'Her name again?'

Sarah spelled both first and last names for him.

When Pavlik finished writing, he looked up. 'What was she doing here?'

'No idea.'

A tap of pen on pad. 'But you do own this building, right?'

He glanced at me for confirmation. I nodded and then, feeling like a traitor, checked sideways on Sarah.

But she didn't seem to be following the thread. 'Brigid was just a kid. I should have looked out for her.'

Sarah had a maternal streak that I never would have believed existed had she not stepped up to become the guardian of two teenagers. When my former partner, Patricia Harper, died, Sarah took her best-friend's kids, Sam and Courtney, into her own home.

I'd say 'and into her heart', too, but Sarah would gag at the sentiment.

Not that it wasn't true.

I had a feeling that the same instinct that drove a single woman in her forties to fight for—and with—two teenagers not her own, was now driving said woman crazy with guilt.

I put my hand on Sarah's and turned to Pavlik. 'Brigid was an apprentice in Sarah's office, but because two other Kingston Realty employees recently…left, Brigid was pretty much on her own.'

Sarah shook off my hand and stood. 'Sheriff, do you think this has anything to do with the other shootings?'

Pavlik cocked his head and even in the spotty lighting I could see the lines of stress in his face. 'Three women dead in the last ten days. All of them real estate agents, though we don't have a cause of death in Ms Ferndale's case. Still, what do you think?'

'Only weren't the other two killed while they were working?' I asked as the technician appeared in the bathroom doorway and signaled to Pavlik.

The sheriff held up a hand to us and approached the other man. After a sotto voce exchange, Pavlik let the techie precede him into the bathroom.

'But Brigid wasn't showing a house,' I said to Pavlik's back. 'She was here, in a room I didn't even know existed.'

His words floated over a shoulder and on toward me. 'Someone sure as hell did.'

SIX

WHEN I TURNED BACK, Sarah was gone.

Alone in the room, I stepped up through the low-bridge doorway and into the daylight. Blinking, I saw no sign of my partner.

I was even more surprised that Ward Chitown, Kate McNamara and Elaine Riordan were also gone. I'd had the lot of them pegged as ambulance chasers, two at least operating under the credentials of investigative journalism.

I still wasn't sure what Elaine Riordan's shtick was.

The area around the base of the platform's staircase had been cordoned off. A sheriff's deputy held up the yellow 'Do Not Cross' tape so I could duck under it and climb the steps.

When I entered Uncommon Grounds, I found Luc Romano tending the counter. Sarah was sitting at a deuce table in the corner. In front of her was coffee that someone, probably Luc, had poured into a latte mug. Sarah was stirring it with a tiny espresso spoon.

'Luc,' I said. 'Thank you so much. How did…?'

'Not a problem,' he said, lavishing the last touch of foam on a cappuccino and tamping the lid of the Styrofoam cup down tightly. A male customer wearing a Bluetooth headset ponied up some bills, looked me over while Luc made change, then left hurriedly.

'Huh,' said Luc. 'Kind of abrupt, even for a coffee-house.'

I shook my head. 'He may have just heard the news. Or gotten a whiff of our air quality.'

A solemn nod. 'I stopped in to invite you and Sarah over to dinner to test out some recipes Tien and I have been developing. When an earlier customer came in, I decided to help out until you got back.'

'Luc, how long ago did you get here?' I asked, glancing at the clocks above our heads.

'Ahh, maybe…an hour?'

Yikes. Between Sarah and me, we didn't have a responsible bone in our bodies. She 'abandons' her apprentice and I…we, abandon our coffeehouse.

I glanced over at my business partner.

Luc lowered his voice. 'She told me what you found downstairs. I figured the best thing to do was leave her alone.'

Good judgment. 'I can't thank you enough, Luc.'

'Like I said, Maggy, happy to help.'

And Tien's father did look happy. More so than ever after both our former locations were destroyed by a freak storm and he'd subsequently decided to retire.

An's Foods, named after Tien's mother, might have been his life, Luc said, but he didn't want it to be his daughter's life as well. Now that Tien had launched her own business, though, 'Dad' was more than happy to help her. And us in the bargain.

Before I could ask what wonders Luc and Tien had whipped up for tonight, the bells on the street-side door jingled.

'What's going on out there?' Art Jenada asked. 'Did someone run into the loading platform this time?'

A car had landed on our front porch just a few months back, so his question wasn't quite the long shot you might imagine.

I told Art about the 'waiting room', but left out for now what—or who—had been found there.

'The mob?' he snorted. 'Not here, not now.'

Sarah stirred at her table, but not with the spoon. Apparently she was actually taking a renewed interest in her surroundings. 'You don't believe the mob was in this area? You're Italian, you should know better.'

Ignoring, for now, the assumption that anyone of Italian descent is an expert on the Mafia, I looked at Art. 'Italian? I thought "Jenada" was Greek?'

'It's neither, but what does my heritage have to do with it?' he demanded, echoing my thoughts.

'Nothing,' I said hastily. 'Nothing at all.'

'The restaurant and slaughterhouse across the tracks were rumored to be mobbed up,' Art continued, 'but the scum, if any, stayed over there where they belonged.'

In my experience, nobody was content staying where they were supposed to belong. In fact, it was the one place that often became intolerable.

I glanced out the platform-side windows in the direction Art was indicating, just in time to see Pavlik stride past. The man did walk with conviction. I just hoped it wasn't Sarah he was interested in convicting.

Luc appeared at my shoulder and cleared his throat. 'Gotta go, Maggy, but we'll see you tonight? Say seven thirty, our place?'

Perfect. That would give me time to run home after we closed and let Frank out.

Frank was my son's sheepdog or, truth be told, now that Eric was away at school, Frank was my sheepdog. He was also, at times, my best friend and most trusted confidante.

'Dinner?' Sarah, my other best friend asked from the table. Food always perked her up.

'Yes,' Luc said, 'and please bring Courtney and Sam.'

'They have after-school stuff,' Sarah said, 'but I'll be there. Thanks, Luc.'

'We'll be glad to see you both,' Tien's father said. 'And Frank, too, if you want, Maggy.'

Pretty sad when your 'plus one' is a four-legged herder of wool on the hoof.

Watching Luc leave, I said, 'I'm sorry, Art.' It was always awkward to discuss an invitation when a listener hadn't been included in, but this was a business dinner of sorts and Art, as a caterer, was competition. 'You were saying?'

But Art was saying nothing because he, too, was gone.

I'M FOND OF categorizing my post-divorce house as 'up the creek'. My ex-husband and I differ on who was left without the proverbial paddle in the divorce settlement.

The creek in question is named Poplar and runs north and south to form the western boundary of Brookhills. The farther downstream you go, the nicer the houses are.

Which is why mine is 'up'.

The outside of the house might be neat-white now,

but when I bought the place it was a grotesque red. Somehow I had been able to see past that—and the overgrown pine trees—to the place's potential. As in, *potentially*, I could afford to live there and still eat. Sadly, with the exception of the ramshackle signal-house near Uncommon Grounds' new location, it might well be the only structure in Brookhills where that was possible.

I'd needed to pay cash, since no bank in its right mind would give a mortgage to a newly divorced woman who had just quit a well-paying corporate job to open a coffeehouse. Oddly enough, the necessity of paying cash had proved to be my salvation during the downturn in the market.

Now I had only my taxes and upkeep to worry about, when many of my neighbors—the ones who had applauded when I painted the eyesore in their midst— were hit with high-interest adjustable loans—or, worse, balloon-payments of principal—coming due for homes that had lost half their value.

They couldn't sell, because they wouldn't get enough from the sale to pay off their mortgages, but they also didn't have enough equity in the homes to negotiate a refinancing.

Talk about your catch-22, more like your catch-22-thousand. Hell, who was I kidding? Add a zero to that for some Brookhillians. Desperate times, and the housing market still wasn't out of the woods.

Parking my 'Sangria Red' Ford Escape in the driveway, I went around to the side and up the steps to my porch. 'Frank? It's me.'

The scrabbling of canine toenails on wood floor.

'Sit,' I commanded through the door.

More scrabbling, then a plop followed by a swish-swish.

Butt on floor, check. Tail wagging, check.

Houston, we have ignition. 'Stay,' I said firmly and put the key in the door.

Clickety-slide,clickety-slide. And it wasn't the key.

It was the sound of a ninety-five-pound sheepdog trying to follow the letter, if not the spirit, of the law.

'No rump-scooting, Frank. You obey, or I won't take you to Luc and Tien's for dinner.'

Woof! Woof-woof-woof!

My mistake, though I wasn't sure if it was the mention of Luc and Tien in particular or 'dinner' in general.

'Sit, Frank!' I ordered again in my best dog-training voice.

Turning the key, I cracked the door. A wet black nose filled part of the space.

'You're supposed to be sitting.'

Sniff.

'Sit, or I'll close the door and leave. You'll have only your sorry furry self to blame.'

We both knew I was bluffing. If I did what I was threatening, I'd return to a urine puddle the size of Lake Michigan and I was down to my last roll of paper towels.

A resigned sigh. Showing Frank who was the alpha dog in this relationship would have to wait. Besides, I feared we both knew the answer.

Flattening myself against the wall next to the door, I reached over and gave the door a shove.

Frank erupted out and down the steps without giving me a look.

But then he didn't knock me over, either.

Victory. Definite, if a bit minor.

WE ARRIVED AT Luc's condo fashionably late, as difficult as it is to be 'fashionably' anything when you're
covered with the sheddings of a sheepdog.

I'd made the mistake of trying to brush Frank after
I showered and got dressed. Never a good idea, especially when you're wearing black, a magnet for dog hair.

Luc's condominium complex, Civic Heights, was
next to Benson Plaza, the strip mall where both the
original Uncommon Grounds and An's Foods had been
located.

The 'Civic' referred to the fact that the condo's entrance faced onto Civic Drive across from the town hall.
The 'Heights' was anybody's guess, though the buildings did ascend heavenward to the highest elevation allowed by code in Brookhills. Four stories.

Luc's place was a two-level townhouse occupying
the first and second floors. I parked on the street behind Tien's Volkswagen bug and Sarah's classic Firebird. As Frank hopped out of my Escape, I was aware
of curious glances. The dogs that were being walked
around us were more the size that would have fit into
Elaine Riordan's handbag, as opposed to Frank, who
was…'Oh, Daddy, look at the pony,' a girl of three or
four said to her dad as they passed. 'Can we get one,
can we please?'

Frank eyed me.

I pressed the doorbell. 'A failure of the educational
system, pooch. In my day, kids could tell the difference
between canines and equines.'

Tien pulled the door open abruptly.

'Sit,' I said to Frank belatedly, but he already was,
tail thumping, as Tien gave him a good rub behind the

ears. 'You're such a perfect gentleman, Frank, aren't you? You're just a lover. Yes you are, oh yes you *are*.'

Ugh. We really had to find somebody for Tien. Maybe Jacque, as unlikely as it seemed, would be the lucky guy.

As for Frank, sheepdogs were like kids. They always behaved better for other people. 'Traitor,' I said as Frank pranced in behind Tien, shooting me a look that said, Now *this* is a woman who knows how to treat a dog.

I closed the door behind me. Beyond the foyer, Luc's condo had a good-sized living room, eat-in kitchen and half-bath. Upstairs were two bedrooms and bathrooms, accessible by a compact circular staircase.

Sarah was already sitting on one end of the couch in the living room, feet up on the coffee table, a glass in her hand.

My partner was a scotch drinker when I met her, but in deference to the medication she took for bipolar disorder, she'd switched to clear liquids.

'Another Grey Goose, Sarah?' asked Luc.

Drinking what she shouldn't—ever the mother, I wanted to scold my partner.

But talking to Sarah was like talking to Frank, currently padding along behind Tien to the kitchen. You could talk, but you never knew if they were listening.

In Frank's case it was because his hair covered his eyes. Sarah just didn't give a shit.

But to my surprise, Sarah shook her head. 'No thanks, Luc. I'm fine for now.'

'Wine, Maggy?' Luc asked, picking up a balloon-shaped glass. 'I've got a nice Chardonnay—that I used making the entrée—or a Cabernet.'

'The Cab, please, Luc.' While I agreed that some dishes were best paired with whites, I fully intended to be drinking the wine both before and after I ate. And I preferred red.

I sniffed. 'Something smells wonderful.'

'Dad developed a fantastic Chicken Francese recipe,' Tien said, re-entering the room with a plate in her hands and my dog at her heels.

She put the plate on the floor and whatever had been on it disappeared in a blur of fur, yellow teeth, pink tongue and consequent drool.

'What was that?' I asked.

'She means before it was barbarically attacked,' said Sarah, nodding toward Frank walking away from the dish, snuffling.

'Meatloaf,' Tien said. 'I hope it's OK?'

'Better than OK,' Sarah said, 'judging by Frank. Got any left? I'm not much for French food.'

I began with, 'Sarah…'

But Luc just laughed. '*Francese* is an Italian word and it means "in the French way", or "Frenchman", literally. You'll see the dish served in a lot of Italian restaurants. Chicken breast, lightly battered in flour and egg and served with a lemon sauce.'

My stomach growled.

'Not only is it delicious,' Luc continued, 'but it should reheat nicely. And I'm doing a nice angel-hair pasta to go with it.'

'Plus,' Tien interjected, 'it's low fat. My father is a culinary genius.'

'Aww, now. Anybody could do this. I've just had the time since I retired.'

'Retired?' I said, settling onto the other end of the couch from Sarah. 'You're developing recipes, helping Tien with the cooking and today you were tending the coffeehouse.'

'You were?' Tien asked with surprise. 'When?'

Of course. She'd been gone by the time Sarah and I had abandoned our post to go in search of what was stinking up the place. Maybe she'd left with Jacque Oui and maybe she hadn't, but I wasn't going to raise the subject.

The Frenchman and Tien's father had been friendly, quasi-competitors, with Jacque running Schultz's, specializing in seafood and fish, just a few blocks from An's, which featured an excellent meat counter, deli and breads.

I didn't know how Luc would feel about Tien seeing Jacque, if that's what they were indeed doing. But Tien was an adult—into her thirties now, though she seemed younger—and who she dated was really none of her father's business.

Or mine, for that matter.

'Around noon, maybe?' Luc, answering Tien's latter question.

'Yeah,' Sarah said, stretching. 'Tien had already taken off with *her* "Francese".'

Meaning Jacque, of course.

'You brought the chicken there?' Luc asked his daughter, confused.

Sarah threw a knowing grin in Tien's direction and then opened her mouth.

I wanted to put my foot in it. Before my partner

could further embarrass Tien, I said to her, 'Your father pitched in when Sarah and I had to leave.'

'Oh, I'm sorry. If I'd known, I would have stayed.' Tien had colored up at Sarah's teasing, but now she seemed to relax, knowing that while I might not be a good influence on Sarah, I was at least a mitigating one.

'Not a problem,' Sarah said, settling back into the couch. 'We just found a corpse in the bathroom of a secret room under the loading dock.'

Tien's hand went to her mouth. 'Was that what the horrible smell was?'

'T'would seem so.' Sarah took a sip of the vodka and then, just when I thought the booze might be muddying her sense of discretion, set it back down. 'Our dead "rat" was my former apprentice, Brigid Ferndale.' Sarah closed her eyes.

Hastily I said, 'The sheriff thinks it might be connected to the other recent attacks on realtors.'

'Then the police believe she was murdered?' Tien asked, eyes wide. 'And why under the…did you say loading platform?'

How to explain? Tien was gone by the time Chitown and his entourage had arrived. She knew nothing of the 'Treasure of the Brookhills Massacre'.

Which I personally thought was a lousy name—sort of a *Treasure of the Sierra Madre* meets *The St Valentine's Day Massacre*. But then, maybe that was what Chitown—or the station grubstaking him—was looking for.

I filled Tien in on the mob 'loot' story, ending with the discovery of the waiting room. 'There was even a shower down there.'

'Probably for cleaning up after whacking people,' Sarah said.

'That was what I—'

'Ridiculous,' Luc exploded. 'No one was "whacking" anyone. Where do you get this stuff?'

As for me, mostly from *The Godfather* trilogy and *The Sopranos*. But it did seem like Luc was overreacting.

He went to a mahogany sideboard with a decanter of amber liquid centered on an old-fashioned white lace doily. His back to us, Luc poured himself several ounces of the liquid. As he raised glass to lips, I remembered.

'Of course,' I said. 'Romano's Ristorante.'

SEVEN

'WHAT ABOUT IT?' Luc had turned abruptly, glass in hand. The drink slopped over the rim, due more to anger than nerves, I thought.

But I also felt cold radiating both from his tone and his face. 'Ward Chitown told me the massacre occurred inside Romano's Ristorante. It's the building on Junction Road and Poplar Creek, just south of the slaughterhouse.'

'The storefront that's been empty for years?' Tien looked at her father, puzzled. 'But isn't that where Pop-Pop's old restaurant and market were, Daddy?'

Sarah: 'Pop-Pop?'

'It's what I call Daddy's—' now Tien was coloring up—'my grandfather. I never knew him because he died before I was born.'

Tien was looking at Luc. When he didn't contribute, she went on. 'My grandmother didn't have the heart to continue with the restaurant after her husband died, so she moved the market to Milwaukee to be closer to her family.'

'Until your dad and mom moved it back to Brookhills,' I said, knowing the story.

Tien's mother, An, had been born in Vietnam. She and Luc, an American soldier, had fallen in love and returned together to the US at the end of his tour of duty. Tragically, when Tien was barely a one-year-old and just after the move to Brookhills, An Romano had been killed in an accident.

Tien's father roused himself. 'My mother gave us the market as a wedding present. I felt bad moving it, but—'

'The business was dying where it was,' Tien chimed in. 'No one was interested in a specialty/butcher shop when they had big chain supermarkets. Daddy decided to bring the store back to Brookhills, where it started and would still be respected.'

'Good place to raise a family,' Luc said, like he'd chanted the maxim a million times before.

'Nona didn't think so,' Tien said.

I said, 'Do you think it was because of—' no need to use the word 'massacre'—'what had happened there?'

Luc hadn't budged from his spot within arm's length of the sideboard.

Sarah said, 'You mean the massacre?'

So much for...

'Is that why Nona never wanted to come to Brookhills, Daddy?' Tien turned to Sarah and me, by way of explanation. 'We always went to Milwaukee. She never once visited us, even at Christmas.'

'Figures,' Sarah said. 'The family business was mobbed up. She didn't want to return to the scene of the crime.'

God, I thought, The US of A was lucky that Sarah never entered our diplomatic corps.

Now Luc shook himself the way my sheepdog Frank would after being out in the rain. 'My father was *not* a gangster.'

'Of course not.' Despite myself, I was intrigued by

what had seemed like ancient history just this morning. Ancient history that had intruded big-time on our current business-plan. 'But from what I understand, a lot of good people have been...' Again, searching for the right word.

'Suckered?' Sarah suggested.

As fitting as any, evil one. But I was Maggy, the Good Bitch of the Midwest. 'Or drawn in, maybe against their will.'

Luc sighed and finally moved, sinking into the chair across from us. Overstuffed and covered with a floral print, it looked as incongruous in the room as Luc did sitting in it. Like a shirt someone dear had bought for him: it didn't suit his taste, but the man simply couldn't bear to give it away.

Tien perched on the arm of the flowered chair. 'Is that what happened? Did Pop-Pop get in bed with the mob?'

To her, it was probably like finding out you were related to Billy the Kid. An unknown and thrilling, if infamous, family history.

To her father, though, the past wasn't quite so...past. 'Don't be melodramatic, Tien. Your grandfather—'

But Sarah couldn't let Tien's comment pass. 'In bed? Like Marlon Brando with the horse's head?'

I cleared my throat. 'Actually, in *The Godfather* it's the movie studio's boss, played by John Marley, who finds the severed—'

'Anyway, *Tien*,' Luc said, leveling a glare at Sarah and me, 'your grandfather owned a restaurant that some reputed Mafia—'

'Reputed?' Sarah said. 'Reputed enough to die in a hail of—'

'Members—' another dirty look from Luc, this time sparing me, but still skewering Sarah—'unfortunately chose to frequent.'

'Were you there the day of the raid?' I asked curiously.

'No, I'd just landed in Vietnam.'

Tien said, 'But Nona and Pop-Pop would have been, right? And customers, of course.'

'It was a Monday. The restaurant was never open on Monday.'

'But the mobsters were there anyway?' Tien followed up before her face changed. 'Oh, I see. That was the reason Pop-Pop closed that day. So nobody would see them.'

'The other way around,' Luc said. 'I think the group chose that day to meet because we were closed. It wasn't unusual in those days.'

'Did you know what was going on?' I asked.

Luc shifted uncomfortably. 'My senior year of high school, I got a whiff of it. My dad going to work, even though the Ristorante wasn't open. I asked why.'

'Did he tell you?' Tien asked.

Luc looked up at her. 'No. And both your Nona and Pop-Pop started to discourage me from stopping by the restaurant on any day.'

'They were trying to keep you safe.' Sarah was staring at her glass.

Luc looked surprised. I was, too, but at Sarah's sensitivity more than the thought that 'Nona' and 'Pop-Pop' wanted to keep their son away from whatever was happening at their place of business.

But Luc had to have seen his parents' motive, too, if only in hindsight. 'It was about then my mom started to encourage me to join the army. The draft was over, but…' His eyes had a faraway look.

I said, 'She must have been very worried about what was going on at their restaurant.'

Tien cocked her head at me. 'Why do you say that, Maggy?'

She deserved an answer. 'A mother suggesting her son enlist while their country's in a shooting war? Sounds like she thought you'd have a better chance at life in Vietnam than at home, Luc.'

'I have to say, I didn't think of it like that back then,' Luc said, patting Tien so she'd shift and he could get up.

He moved to the sideboard and poured himself another drink from the decanter. 'I figured she and my father thought I could use some toughening up.'

Nothing like dodging bullets to put starch in your shorts. But I was thinking along a different line. Tien had said her grandfather died before she was born, but he apparently had been alive back when Luc enlisted.

'Another question?' I said.

'Really?' Luc settled back into the chair with his refilled glass. 'I think I've answered plenty. Sure more than I ever hoped to.' He gave his daughter a weary smile.

I said, 'You told us the restaurant wasn't open the day of the FBI's raid. But you also said your father started working on Mondays. So…was he there?'

'Did Pop-Pop see what happened?' Tien asked. Like

me, she seemed intrigued by this new window into her heritage.

'I only know what your grandmother told me.' Luc's hazel eyes met those of his daughter's. Exact same color, but Tien's with an Asian lift at the corners. 'Your grandfather was killed that day by an FBI bullet.'

EIGHT

'But you said Pop-Pop wasn't in the Mafia.' Tien's beautiful eyes teared up. 'Why did they shoot him?'

'It was an accident, sweetie,' Luc said. 'The authorities kicked in the door and guns on both sides started blazing. It could just as easily have been one of the mob lieutenants who fired the round that killed my father.'

Probably hard to tell the good guys from the bad, under those circumstances. And, though I wouldn't say it aloud, Tien's father *had* harbored criminals in his restaurant. Knowingly, repeatedly and, from what Luc had said, without anybody putting a gun to his head.

'But the bullet did come from an FBI gun?'

Luc shrugged. 'According to my mother, though I'm not sure how reliable she ever was on the subject. She'd only talk about it when she drank homemade wine and had filled up the jelly jar enough times to get morose.'

Jelly jars made into glasses. I remembered a tiny hole-in-the-wall Italian restaurant in Milwaukee that had made their own wine and served it in Welch's Flintstones jelly jars.

'Did your mother resent the FBI?' I asked.

'No.' Luc alternatingly clenched and relaxed his free hand. 'She resented my father for getting involved with somebody called Little Mo, one of the gangsters killed that day.'

Tien, who had retaken her spot on the arm of his chair, twisted to regard him. 'You seem to know an awful lot about the Mafia. Are you sure—'

'Don't worry, sweetie. I just did some research because I was curious.' He punched her lightly on the arm. 'As you should understand.'

'Like father like daughter, I guess,' Tien said, then her eyes darkened. 'But have you told me everything? No more surprises? I won't find out my great-great-great grandfather was Attila the Hun or something?'

'Promise,' Luc said, holding up his free hand. 'Now is everyone ready for dinner?'

It was after nine when we'd finally sat down to eat, Sarah having taken a little snooze as the rest of us put dinner on the table.

'That was delicious,' I said to Luc as he passed me my jacket. 'I think the Chicken Francese will be a perfect addition to our Prepared Food section.'

'We just have to make sure we don't overcook it,' Tien said. 'Otherwise it will dry out when it's reheated.'

'Maybe we should put instructions on it,' Luc said to his daughter. 'It really would be best sautéed just enough to crisp up the breading and heat through.'

Sarah, who had her hand on the doorknob, snorted. 'Sauté it? Please, if you can't order it fresh—or at least nuke it back to life—nobody's going to eat it anyway.'

'That's you and me, Sarah,' I said, pushing her ahead of me out the door. 'Takeout and microwave dinners. Most people in Brookhills have gorgeous gourmet kitchens.'

I waved goodbye to Luc and Tien, who was staying behind to help her dad clean up.

'Doesn't mean those people cook in 'em.'

Sarah being a case in point. Lovely house, beautifully appointed kitchen, layer of dust on most appliances.

I said, 'Are you all right to drive?'

'Of course. I had just the one vodka and that was three hours ago.'

Not to mention a big meal and nap, though not in that order. We had reached the sidewalk. 'Were you drinking because of...?'

'Brigid?' Sarah had her key out and was walking to her yellow 1975 Firebird, yet another item dating from the mid-seventies. 'No.'

She stopped and turned. 'Not that I'm letting myself off the hook. Brigid was my responsibility as surely as Sam and Courtney are.'

'You are those kids' legal guardian.'

'I had a legal responsibility to Brigid, too.' Sarah examined the keys in her hand. 'Thing was, Maggy, the kid looked and acted more mature than she really was. I guess I just bought into it. Let her make decisions that should have been mine and mine alone. Partly because I was older, but mostly because I was the fully-accredited and licensed boss. I screwed up.'

'It's not your fault she's dead. You didn't—'

'You're right, I didn't.' My partner stuck her key in the door of her classic car. 'I didn't teach her how to stay safe. I didn't show her the articles on the broker websites about dangerous situations.'

'You told her not to show houses alone.'

'But, like you said, who would she have taken? Who would have called her to make sure she was OK?'

Now Sarah was using my words to make *her* point.

She swung her door open and slid in. 'I never met any of her friends and she was all alone in the office. I fired everyone else, remember?'

'You are *not* a bad person,' I protested.

She turned her key in the ignition. 'Maybe, but I'm not a good one, either.' Then Sarah slammed her driver's door shut, gunned the engine and drove away.

'You are, too,' I said to the receding tail lights. Maybe not a *nice* person, but Sarah in her own way was good-hearted. She just…well, buried it under a load of defensive crap.

I tweet-tweeted the Escape's key fob to open my door and got in.

I was worried about my partner. 'Bipolar disorder' was jargon for what once was simply and descriptively called 'manic depression'. Thanks to the meds, Sarah's manic phase seemed controlled, but I wasn't sure what accumulation of grief would tip her over into depression.

Pavlik hadn't liked that Sarah's employee was found dead, and under Sarah's building. It wouldn't take him long to discover the complaint Brigid had lodged with the state against her employer.

And then what?

When Sarah had opened that envelope—Brigid's corpse practically beneath our feet—she'd been shocked. Blindsided.

And even if Sarah had been aware of the complaint

before then, she certainly wouldn't kill somebody over it and stash the body on her own property.

Ridiculous. I knew it and I'd make sure Pavlik did, too.

I started the Escape, feeling more confident. Of course, I could help my friend. I was capable, I was responsible. I...

'Yoo-hoo, Maggy?' Tien was in the doorway. 'You forgot something.'

Frank came bounding toward the car.

NINE

THE NEXT MORNING I was bouncing around the tiny house like a pinball, but it was just habit. Out of bed and into the bathroom, down the hall to the kitchen to start the coffee, back to take a shower, then half-dressed to the laundry room in hopes of finding a clean Uncommon Grounds T-shirt, quick detour for coffee on the way to the bathroom to redeem a 'gently worn' shirt from the hamper, back to the kitchen to fill Frank's food bowls and my travel mug, a search of the living room for my keys.

And every time I entered a room, Frank left it.

'I told you I was sorry,' I said as he pushed himself up from the floor in front of the unlit fireplace and walked stiff-legged into the hallway.

'Not that you shouldn't share some of the blame,' I called after him. 'If you hadn't scarfed down all Tien's meat loaf, you wouldn't have become so logy that you fell asleep on Luc's bed.'

I still didn't see how the plus-sized sheepdog had made it up the circular staircase. Though it might explain Frank's creakiness—in addition to his crankiness—this morning.

The big galoot probably pulled something.

'Fine, sulk if you want,' I said, catching sight of my car keys on the chair by the door. 'I have to get to work. Someone in this house needs to do more than eat and sleep.'

OK, add pee and poop, though I always remained hopeful that, at least for Frank, these last two would be exterior operations.

Walking out into the cold morning, I thought about how my life had changed from three years ago, when I had a husband and a son, a prestigious job in corporate PR and a big house.

And no pets.

Today I was divorced, with my son away at college and my fledgling shop struggling. My house was small and my sheepdog was large.

Oh, and I talked to him. A lot.

Not that I wasn't happy, you understand. It was just… yeah, 'different' captured it well enough.

I had a sudden surge of loneliness and thought about calling Eric at the University of Minnesota. As I turned the key in the Escape, the time flashed 8:09. Nope. Just into his third year, he had an early class and the last thing I wanted to do was make him late.

The last couple of years had been tough on Eric, both because of Ted's and my divorce and Eric's own realization that he, himself, was gay. Our son had told me and then his father and, relieved that we loved him and life wasn't going to come crashing down around him—at least, more than it already had with the divorce—Eric had gone back to the 'U'.

A huge relief because, though Ted was responsible for Eric's tuition, my ex and I shared joint custody of a fervent desire to see our son graduate. And be happy.

I drove the short distance to Uncommon Grounds

and pulled into the parking lot. Leaving the Escape, I moved around the track side of the building. The area that had been cordoned off yesterday still was, guarded by only one sheriff's deputy next to the steps.

I said good morning and he nodded back, an Uncommon Grounds to-go cup in his left hand.

'Can I get you a refill?'

'No, thank you, ma'am. Amy just brought me this one.'

'Great,' I said as I started up the stairs to the platform. 'Just yell if you need anything.'

I stopped and craned my neck down to see him. 'Do you happen to know if Sheriff Pavlik will be by today?'

The hint of a grin, quickly stifled. That Pavlik was dating the local Typhoid Mary of untimely deaths was common knowledge, not that the department respected its sheriff any less. I wasn't quite sure what his troops thought of me.

'He's inside, ma'am,' the deputy replied, nodding toward the door behind the steps. 'Would you like to speak with him?'

I did, though not necessarily in front of one of his subordinates. 'No, thanks, I'll—'

'Maggy.' Pavlik emerged from the half-door to the waiting room below. 'A moment?'

'Certainly.' I backtracked down the steps and ducked under the tape, avoiding the deputy's eyes. It felt uncomfortably close to being summoned to the principal's office.

Pavlik moved aside to let me enter, then followed me down the two steps to the linoleum floor. In contrast to yesterday when he might have been dressed for court, today Pavlik was relatively casual. Dark-wash jeans and a dress shirt with the cuffs folded up. So simple and yet so, so…

I glanced behind me to see if the deputy had stayed close, but the coast was clear. 'Permission to approach the sheriff, sir?'

The crinkle lines at the corners of his eyes showed the smile his mouth didn't. 'Permission denied.'

'So put me in jail.' I stood on tiptoe and kissed him on the lips.

His hand came up to steady me at the waist and with a groan he pulled me into him. 'I've missed you, Maggy.'

'Me, too.' Twining my arms around his neck, I hung there for a second and then stepped back. We both knew it wouldn't do for the county sheriff to be canoodling at a murder scene.

'We're going to secure the door and keep the area taped,' Pavlik said, looking tired, 'but Harris out there will be taking off once the crime scene guys are done.'

'That's fine.' I shook my head. 'Poor Brigid. How horrible to take your last breaths in there.' I tilted my head toward the stuffy little bathroom. 'And all alone to boot. She was beautiful and young, not much older than Eric. She should have been out having fun, not…'

'Dying? I agree. But from what we've determined so far, she wasn't killed here.'

'No?' I struggled to embrace the first arguably good news I'd had without jinxing it.

'Ms Ferndale was hit in the back of the head.' Pavlik used his right hand as a teacher's aide. 'And wherever that happened, there should have been a good amount of blood.'

'But there wasn't,' I said, glancing toward the bathroom. Since Brigid had been face-up, I couldn't have seen the wound without moving her body, not only bad crime-scene behavior but just plain yucky. I certainly didn't recall any blood, though, much less 'a good amount'.

'But, Pavlik, if Brigid was killed somewhere else, how did she get here?'

'Good question.'

'Could she have been injured, but not realizing how badly? You know, internal bleeding?'

'The brain or skull, you mean? Not likely. The deceased bled out, but somewhere else.' He sagged down onto the couch.

'You look exhausted. Did you get any sleep last night?'

Pavlik ran his hand through his curly hair. 'Not much. The other two killings were real estate agents working alone. I was leaning toward someone with a grudge.'

'Some kind of vendetta?' I sat down next to him, thinking how melodramatic it all sounded for Brookhills.

'A lot of people have lost their homes, Maggy. They're angry, and the closest "messenger" around is probably a realtor.'

As in 'don't kill the messenger'. Except someone had.

But I knew Pavlik was right about feelings running high. One of our customers had bought a house at foreclosure, only to have it nearly destroyed by the original homeowner. Sad on both counts—the people who lost their home, but also my young customer. He'd finally scraped enough money together to buy a house, only to put thousands more into it to repair the damage.

Everybody loses.

I said, 'Angry and frustrated, I understand, but… killing your real estate agent?'

'Real estate agents, bankers, the person who's buying your house out from under you. When you've lost everything…'

'…you have nothing left to lose,' I finished for him. 'You said you *were* leaning toward someone with a grudge. Have you changed your mind?'

'Only in the number of people who might be involved.' Pavlik stood back up, the frustration exhibited by his restlessness getting the better of him. 'This killing is different, though. Blunt force trauma to the back of the head instead of a bullet through the temple.'

'Two different methods, two different killers?' I mulled it over. 'But the methods are similar in that the attacker had to be close-in. Didn't you tell me there was stippling?'

Stippling—almost a tattoo on and under the skin caused by the unburned gunpowder of a shot at close-range. I might not know pistols from revolvers, but I did watch crime-scene TV.

'Some irregular stippling on both gunshot victims. Almost like something had blocked part of it.'

'Another attacker, maybe holding the victim?'

'Perhaps, Sherlock,' Pavlik said, with the ghost of a grin. 'But if you see someone with weird powder burns, call me. No heroics.'

Since I'm about as far from hero material as you can get, I agreed. Mostly I take chances because I'm scared witless. 'So an accomplice would explain the odd stippling, as well as the variation in method.'

'Not to mention moving the body. It likely took two people. Brigid Ferndale wasn't a big woman, but...well, she was a dead weight, in the very literal sense of the term.'

I gave a shiver and Pavlik pulled me close. 'I have to get back to work.'

I hung on. 'Be careful.'

'I could say the same to you,' he murmured in my hair. 'I don't like it when bodies are found around people I care for.'

'You and me both. Though we probably should be used to it by now.'

Pavlik put one hand on each of my shoulders and held me at arms' length, so he could see my face. 'Understand one thing, Maggy. I will never get "used to" your being in danger.'

'But I'm not in danger. You said yourself that Brigid wasn't killed in the depot.' Pavlik towering a half-foot over me, I tried to stand on tiptoes to kiss him.

He wouldn't let me. 'Someone moved the corpse here for a reason.'

'Understood.' The concept, if not the reason that he was talking about.

Pavlik kissed me properly before letting me go. 'I have to go look for a primary crime scene. With a blood pool.'

Lovely image. 'How will you find it, though? Thanks

to the economy, there have to be hundreds—if not thousands—of empty properties in the county.'

He shrugged. 'We might be able to narrow our search field by tracking the deceased's movements during her last day. Her parents are divorced and Ms Ferndale lived with her mother, who told me her daughter called Monday afternoon, saying she was going out to a club and wouldn't be back until late.'

That fit with what Brigid had been wearing when we'd found her. 'But she never got home?'

Sheriff Jake Pavlik shook his head. 'And now she never will.'

LEAVING HIM, I continued up the stairs, mentally slapping myself upside the head for not making a phone call last night.

Amy, our lead barista, would have arrived this morning to find police tape and a deputy stationed. With everything that had gone on yesterday, I'd completely forgotten to fill her in. I doubted that Sarah had thought of it, either.

But true to form, Amy had taken it all in stride and even gotten the deputy coffee. God, we were lucky to have her.

In the barista pantheon, Amy Caprese was a rock star. Brightly hued hair, multiple piercings, tats and a kick-ass knack for marketing. She'd even come up with our new logo—a stylized espresso machine that resembled a locomotive. You got 'coffee' and 'train' melded into a single glance.

Genius. And she deserved better from her employers. In a real coup, my former partner Caron and I had lured Amy away from a competing coffeehouse. Now, with the addition of Tien and occasionally Luc, Sarah and I had built a full staff. And a crackerjack one at that.

With the last commuter train of the morning already chugging toward Milwaukee and no Barbies—tennis, broker, Malibu or otherwise—as yet arriving, the only person in the place was a man who looked like a grad student. He was sitting at the counter where he could plug in his notebook computer.

Amy was wiping tables and straightened up when I came in. Her hair looked like Fruit Stripe Gum. I didn't comment on it: a waste of breath, since tomorrow's do would be different anyway.

'I am so sorry, Amy,' I said. 'I meant to call and warn you about all this.'

'Not a problem.' Amy flapped the dishcloth in her hand. 'I caught the TV news last night.'

'I didn't. What did they say?' I asked.

'Just that the body of a woman had been discovered under the platform.'

'They didn't identify her?'

'No, but Tien told me it was Brigid Ferndale. What in the world could she have been doing under there?'

'You knew Brigid?'

'Yes, from Sapphire,' Amy said, moving to the condiment cart. 'In fact, I'm not sure I was ever there when she wasn't. Quite the party girl.'

Sapphire.

Brigid told her mother she was going clubbing the night she'd disappeared and Sapphire was just across the county line between Milwaukee and Brookhills. The dance place drew young professionals from both counties, as well as local media types, sports figures, etc. In other words, anyone who was anyone.

Or wanted to *be* anyone. Or wanted to *do* anyone who was anyone. Or *become*…well, you get the picture.

'Sapphire?' I repeated. It wasn't that Amy didn't belong in a place that catered to the beautiful people. She was beautiful in an offbeat, interesting way. 'That doesn't seem to be your…'

'Scene?' Amy completed for me. 'It's not, though it *is* fascinating people-watching. I've spent a lot of time there lately because the club is going green and hired me to do some consulting.'

Ah, now that made sense. Amy was involved in a number of environmental groups in the area and had spearheaded an effort to encourage local coffeehouses and restaurants to use Fair Trade and shade-grown coffees.

'Fair Trade' beans were certified to have been grown in a way that was environmentally friendly and also provided decent wages for the people in the fields. Shade-grown efforts helped to preserve forests that would otherwise be clear-cut in order to plant coffee.

Uncommon Grounds, of course, used both. Or Amy would have clear-cut *us*.

Then there was the worst-case scenario: Amy could just quit. She could survive—hell, thrive—beyond the walls of Uncommon Grounds, but it couldn't survive without her.

I waved her to a table. 'What can you tell me about Brigid?'

Amy sat, draping her cloth over the back of a chair and glancing over at the grad student before she leaned forward. 'You *do* know that Brigid worked at Kingston Realty, right?'

I nodded. 'Yes, but how do you know?'

Amy shifted in her seat. 'Brigid was spreading the word that she was unhappy and looking for a new "opportunity". Said Sarah was taking advantage of her good nature. Such as it was.'

'I'm getting the impression Brigid wasn't such a nice person.'

'Depended. She was *real* nice to guys with money or fame. Or anyone, either sex, that Brigid thought could get her what she wanted.'

'Which was?'

'Anything and everything. Brigid struck me as a social climber who would scrabble over anybody to reach the ladder's top.'

The way Amy said it made me think she had personal experience. 'Was she "nice" to you because she wanted something?'

Amy shrugged. 'Brigid asked about Uncommon Grounds and Sarah and you. At the time, I had the feeling she was looking for dirt.'

And had found it in her own backyard—Sarah's admitted negligence in training her. And now Brigid had been killed and dumped in *our* backyard. But why?

'But,' Amy shifted uncomfortably, 'now that she's dead, I hate…'

'…to speak ill of the dead?' I finished for her. 'Sometimes that's the only way to find out why someone died.'

'I suppose.' She chewed on that for a second. 'I understand her body was found under the loading platform?'

'Believe it or not, there's a furnished space under

there with electricity—even a bathroom.' I didn't mention that it was in that small room Brigid was found.

'Why in the world would anyone go to all that trouble? Did it predate the depot here?' She held out her hand, palm up.

'This building is 150 years old,' I said. 'The room we're talking about looks pure 1970s. I think the only ones who ever used it were mobsters, preserving their privacy until the train to their destination arrived.'

'Seriously?' Amy asked, her eyes round. 'That is so cool.'

'Cooler', perhaps, if it had happened under someone else's coffeehouse, but I got her point. To people Amy and Tien's age and even mine, gangsters were the subjects of movies and television. There for entertainment value, not to be feared.

'I guess it makes sense,' Amy continued. 'What with the Ristorante being right across the way.'

'You know about it being used by the Mafia?'

'Of course. It's Brookhills lore.'

I'd lived here all of my married—and now divorced—life and I didn't know Brookhills *had* any lore. Of course, I'd spent a lot of those years working long hours in downtown Milwaukee.

'The shoot-out, the *consigliere* who got away with the money,' Amy was saying, 'I used to pretend he fell in love with me and we ran away together.'

'You weren't born yet,' I said. 'And, besides, he was a criminal.'

'Didn't matter. We were studying La Cosa Nostra in school and I'd been doing a little independent reading. Mario Puzo's *The Godfather* and—'

'Let me guess,' I said. 'Page twenty-three.'

Amy wrinkled her nose. 'It was twenty-six, I thought, though I suppose that would depend on the edition. But you get my drift.'

I did, as apparently my mother had as well. It was her copy of the novel I'd found, the spine forever cracked to the page where Sonny Corleone and his sister's bridesmaid do the dirty.

Ahh, tradition. But that's another movie.

'Well, it's not quite *The Godfather*,' I said, 'but Ward Chitown seems to think there will be interest in his production.'

'Chitown?' Amy repeated. 'There was something about him in…'

She reached over and snagged a stack of newspapers, sifting through them until finding the one she wanted. The thing had been folded inside out, so it took her a second to smooth it out on the table.

Amy pointed. Saturday morning. Page 1, and above the fold. 'Hunt for Brookhills loot goes prime-time,' was the headline.

I pulled the paper toward me and read aloud. '"Some twenty-five years after Geraldo Rivera's *The Mystery of Al Capone's Vault*, Ward Chitown is betting his own treasure hunt will yield higher dividends."'

Amy seemed puzzled. 'Al Capone's vault?'

'I actually saw Geraldo's special on TV,' I said. 'A construction company renovating the Lexington Hotel in Chicago stumbled on a series of tunnels and a vault of some kind. Rivera had just been fired from ABC and he hosted this program, trying to revive his career. You should have heard the hype. A two-hour live show, with the medical examiner there in case they found bodies and the IRS in case they found money.'

'And?'

'Beyond some empty bottles, they found squat.'

'That's all?'

'Yup. But thirty million people watched. 1986.'

'Wow. So that was the first reality show—before *The Real World* or *Survivor*, even.'

'I never thought of it like that,' I said. 'But you're right. And it was spellbinding, until the final reveal. I guess we all should have realized that reality shows had found their John the Baptist.'

Amy studied the paper. 'The article doesn't mention the space under the platform. It sounds like Chitown thinks the money is somewhere in the restaurant or slaughterhouse.'

'He didn't know about the so-called "waiting room". Besides, the whole thing is a bunch of hooey.'

Amy blinked. 'Hooey?'

'You know, nonsense.'

'I know what the word means, Maggy. I just never heard it actually spoken in real life before. So why do you think we're in…hooey territory?'

'Because if the money was stashed more than thirty-five years ago, surely someone would have found it by now.'

Amy frowned. 'I'm not convinced. After all, they didn't find your "waiting room". Besides, everyone assumed my dreamboat mobster got away with it. Now Chitown…ohhh.' Her facial expression changed.

'What?'

'This quotes an anonymous source who maintains

that skeletal remains found at the state line may actually have belonged to this *consigliere* wounded in the attack and trying to make it back to Chicago.'

Amy looked heartbroken.

I said, 'You do realize that whether the man was killed that day or not, he'd be at least sixty-five or seventy today. A little old for you and, besides, he'd have spent most of that money by now, with just petty cash left over to buy adult diapers and all.'

I was being facetious, but Amy's eyes went round.

'You're right—it was only a million it says here and it's been thirty-seven years. That's what? $27,000 and change a year?'

Can't say our barista didn't have excellent math skills. 'Good point. The police shouldn't be looking for the guy at the state line. They should be checking the greeters at Wal-Mart.'

'I hear it's not a bad job, except for the customers.' Amy seemed to shift gears. 'You know, this could be a huge opportunity.'

'For what?'

'For us.' She stared at me. 'The gangster connection's just been dropped in our laps. You know, sub-machine guns, violin cases.'

'This was the seventies, not the thirties,' I said. 'Al Capone did *not* sip here.'

'A shame,' my star barista said. 'It's got a nice ring to it. But it not being Capone—though I bet he stepped on or off a train here at some point—doesn't mean we can't make the most of what *did* happen. Like theme drinks. How about a triple-shot mob-uccino?'

'Clever. Though in questionable taste, maybe, given

that a woman's body was just found under our place of business. A victim, who, by the way, worked for said coffeehouse's co-owner. We don't want people to think we're exploiting someone else's misfortune.'

Wait a minute. Dear God, did I just call having your head cracked open a 'misfortune'?

'Totally dead-on, Maggy. It would be unseemly to launch something too soon. We should hold off at least a week.'

I was still trying to get past 'totally dead-on'.

'Maggy?'

'You're right. We should wait a week. Or longer.' Like a decade.

Amy brightened. 'You're a genius at public relations, you know that? I'm pretty good at marketing, but you have your finger on the pulse of the people.'

At least *sane* people, though that may be because I work with so few of them I go out of my way to impress those I do come across.

Amy was tapping her raspberry fruit-stripe now. 'You know what I'm worried about, though?'

The henna hair dye eating away through scalp, then skull, and finally brain? 'No. What?'

'That in the process of being sensitive, we miss out on the wave of interest Chitown's show might create.'

I hate to admit it, but except for the body in the basement, I could be in our barista-cum-marketer's corner on this. It would be fun to build the business around a theme.

Amy stood up. 'Do you think that's why Brigid was in the waiting room? Looking for treasure?'

'How would she know the room even existed?'

Through trial and error—literally, on both counts—
I'd found it wasn't a good idea to share anything I got
from Pavlik unless he expressly told me I could. The
probability that Brigid had been killed somewhere else
and moved was something I needed to keep to myself
for now. 'You said it's not mentioned in the news article.'

'Well then, maybe Brigid came up with independent sources. You know, like Sarah. After all, Kingston Realty has the listing for that whole block across
the tracks.'

'Including Roma… I mean, the one where the FBI
raid took place?' Sarah sure hadn't shared that factoid
with me. 'How do you know that?'

'Romano's is the name of the restaurant.' Amy staying casual, either not seeing the connection to Luc and
Tien or not caring. 'Part of Brigid's rant about Sarah was
that Kingston Realty had held the listing for years. And
the woman Brigid was speaking to said—her words
not mine—"anyone who knew her ass from a hole in
the wall should have sold the property ten times over
by now".'

'Sarah being the owner of the ass in question?'

Amy nodded. ''Fraid so.'

My turn to ponder. 'Was this Monday night, by any
chance?'

'Monday? No, this was last week. I can check my
calendar, if you like, because I had a meeting with Mi-
chael, Sapphire's manager. That's why I was sitting
there eavesdropping.'

'Did you know the woman with Brigid?' Less important, since the conversation hadn't taken place the night
Brigid had disappeared. Still, the information might

lead somewhere. And that somewhere might be an itch Pavlik hadn't scratched.

'Maggy, I've seen her right here in Uncommon Grounds, though just occasionally, so I don't recall her name. But she's a Barbie.'

'Tennis or soccer mom? Blonde, brunette or red-head?'

Animal, vegetable or mineral?

'Redhead, I think,' Amy said. 'Though it's hard to be sure with the lights in Sapphire. Sometimes they make my hair look blue.'

Amy, honey, sometimes your hair *is* blue.

But if the woman Brigid had been talking to was a redhead, she couldn't have been any of the Barbies I'd seen yesterday. One brunette and three blondes. Pretty much the demographic in Brookhills, where you'd swear blonde was the magically dominant gene.

'I'm not placing her,' I said.

'Not surprising, Maggy,' Amy said with a smile. 'The only time you actually look at our customers is when you're evaluating them for jail time.'

'Is that true?' I said, a little shocked. Not at myself, necessarily, so much that Amy had noticed. My mind did tend to wander when I was working my shift.

'Maybe not the jail part, literally. But you're not much of a people person.'

'In fairness,' I said, 'my original partners Patricia and Caron were supposed to be the "people" people. I was more the planner and marketer. When Patricia died and Caron called it quits, Sarah—'

'Who, in my humble opinion, is better with the cus-tomers than you are.'

'Is not.' Drive a dagger through my heart, why don't you? 'Sarah is…is insulting at best. Caustic even.'

'Granted, but at least she talks to them.' Amy plucked her dishcloth from the back of the chair. 'Anything else I can do for you, Maggy? I promised Tien I'd package the soup into carry-out containers once it cooled.'

'Nope,' I said, picking myself up in more ways than one. 'Hey, Amy?'

'Yes?'

'When was the last time you saw Brigid Ferndale at Sapphire?'

Our barista stopped at the door to the kitchen. 'The last time? Just a couple of days ago. Monday night, maybe?'

Bingo. The night Sarah's apprentice was killed.

Time for a little off-campus people-watching of my own.

TEN

MEANING THAT I, Maggy Thorsen, was going clubbing. I thought about asking Amy to accompany me, as her shift ended at noon. Truth be told, though, I was still smarting from my employee's low opinion of her boss.

Not a 'people person', my ass.

I was kind of hoping to go right from work—sort of a dance club version of your early-bird special—but Sapphire's outgoing message told me the place's doors didn't even open until 10 p.m.

Which gave me plenty of time to close the shop and go home to patch things up with the indignant Frank before dining together. And, finally, shower/make-up/dress-up.

After Amy left, I put a call in to Sarah. She hadn't returned it, so I went out to see if the sheriff's deputy guarding the waiting room door needed lunch, but he was gone, as Pavlik had predicted. The only vestige of what had happened there was the yellow crime-scene tape that still sashed the door.

By 2:30, I was sitting at our counter with a pad of white, lined paper in front of me when MaryAnne and two other women came through our street-side jingle-door.

I stood up to serve the trio, thinking that if I kept

finding bodies around the depot, a 'The Bell Tolls for Thee' signature might be more appropriate.

One of the women was the brunette with MaryAnne yesterday, but the other was neither Elaine Riordan nor the other blonde.

This was a redhead. Of course—Gabriella Atherton, owner of the new real estate office in town and Sarah's prime rival for any upscale properties. 'Broker Barbie', in Sarah's mind, but I feared she could be underestimating the woman.

More in the current context, though, was it Gabriella Atherton that Amy saw Brigid Ferndale speaking with at Sapphire? Looking back on what our barista had overheard, it seemed likely that Brigid's companion was a fellow agent capable of picking apart Sarah and her abilities. And, as a broker herself, Gabriella Atherton could offer Brigid a desk in the redhead's own office.

As simple as that, though? Competing broker luring apprentice and future employee away from status quo? Or, given what I'd heard about Brigid, was the apprentice selling out my Sarah to become part of a newer, hipper agency?

And one with more than an absentee mentor on board.

'Ladies, you're late,' I said. 'I was afraid we wouldn't see you today.'

'Now don't you worry, honey,' MaryAnne said. 'Georgia had an emergency appointment after lunch—'

Atherton interjected, 'How do you break a nail using chopsticks, I ask you?'

But MaryAnne plowed onward. 'Be that as it may, Maggy, the rest of us you can't shake loose with a stick.'

Remember the Amy, if not the Alamo. People-person, people-person.

'Tennis and lunch—what a nice day.' I sounded phony even to my own ears, but I was trying.

'Honey, you don't even know the half of it,' Mary-Anne said with a broad grin. 'You see, our league had a special, very special, Thursday round-robin? Followed by lunch with the opposing team, of course.'

Of course.

'Losers.' Gabriella Atherton tucked a lock of auburn hair behind one ear. Up close, she looked to be mid-thirties—more than a full decade *older* than Brigid, but about the same number of years *younger* than Sarah. Which probably didn't please my business partner either.

'Honestly,' the brunette said, sitting down heavily. 'That waiter was so inefficient. You'd think no one had ever asked for separate checks before. I can't imagine whatever took so long.'

Let's see. Two teams of eight, maybe ten women, all persnickety about their calorie-counts and each demanding salad dressing on the side and a separate check. That's a whole lot of artificially-sweetened iced tea to spit in.

'Inexcusable,' I said chirpily. 'Now what can I get you?'

'I'll have an iced mocha,' Atherton said. 'Light on the ice.'

She turned to the brunette. 'It just goes against my grain to pay for frozen water. Sometimes I get an iced mocha that's not.'

'Not iced? But isn't it warm?'

'The espresso is warm,' said Atherton, 'but Maggy here takes care of me.'

She favored me with the Atherton smile, made famous by her most recent billboard campaign to establish her new agency, yard signs considered déclassé in Brookhills. Why hadn't I been able to dredge up her name when Amy had described a redheaded Barbie?

Honest answer? I'd never noticed Gabriella Atherton in Uncommon Grounds before—this, despite the fact that I'd obviously served her in the past.

'Maggy just mixes the espresso with cold milk,' Atherton was saying, 'and then I take it back to the office and pour it over ice there. I get almost twice as much that way.'

The woman drove a high-end Mercedes and owned the hottest real estate company in town, yet she was feeling triumphant over wringing an extra half-cup of milk out of struggling little me. Lovely.

Then again, she did remember my name.

'But you did tell me you wanted some ice today, *Gabriella*?' I smiled. Take that, Amy Caprese.

'Yes, please.' A hesitation. 'Oh, wait, Maggy. Can you make it an iced latte, instead of a mocha? With whole milk.'

'Whole milk?' The brunette voiced the kind of horror I reserved for things Frank coughed up on the carpet.

'Ohhh, you're right,' Atherton said, patting her artfully flat abdominals. 'Maggy, best make it skim, then. With one Splenda, as usual.'

'Of course.' I made an effort to file away the 'usual' no-ice/one Splenda for future reference, though I feared Amy was right.

I just didn't give a shit.

'And don't forget: that's light on the ice.'

'Gotcha.'

'I'm surprised you aren't busier, Maggy,' from the brunette. I really had to find out what her name was. 'I mean, what with the poor woman dying in your cellar. You know what gossipmongers some folks can be. Waaay—' this accompanied by an eye roll—'too much time on their hands.'

Sayeth the woman who took a two-hour athletic endeavor, added a social luncheon and topped it off with coffee out with friends.

During her last sentence, Brunette glanced around the room, hoping, I thought, to spot some mongers she could gossip about later.

'The entrance to the room where she was found is outside,' I said. 'Sealed by police tape and everything.'

Brunette blushed. 'Just a black coffee for me, please.'

'Coming up.' I brewed Gabriella Atherton's espresso shot so it could cool down as I poured the other woman's coffee.

From behind me came Atherton's voice. 'The Mafia connection with Brookhills is just absolutely fascinating. I had no idea when I moved to our little fly-speck of a town that its history was so colorful.'

'Or that you would find the love of your life.' This from Brunette. For her part, MaryAnne was standing nearby, paging through a magazine from our newsstand.

'This chapter of it, certainly,' Atherton said. 'But life is a book with many leaves still to be turned.'

'Chick-lit, no doubt,' I heard MaryAnne mumble under her breath.

Atherton apparently didn't hear her. Or chose not to. 'Robert and I have booked the Wisconsin Club's Grand Ballroom for June.'

'June? And on such short notice?' Brunette, again. 'Robert must have had to pull an awful lot of strings.'

'Not Robert, really.' Atherton seemed miffed. 'It was all my doing, actually.'

'Oh, I'm *so* sorry, Gabriella,' Brunette said, as though she'd just accidentally lopped off an Atherton forearm with a negligently wielded machete. 'I just thought that Robert, being from here and having been married once at the Wis—' She slapped her mouth shut.

'Not to worry, Jane,' said Atherton, seeming to mellow when confronted with the gaffe of a lesser Barbie, 'I knew perfectly well that Robert and his ex were married at the Wisconsin Club, but I have no intention of letting that historical coincidence prevent me from choosing the venue I want for my reception.'

'Very wise of you,' said Brunette—or, hereafter, Jane. 'Oh, Maggy. Could you put just a smidge of steamed milk in my coffee?'

'Of course.' I pulled back the cup I'd started to slide to her and set the milk to steam.

'And half a packet of Splenda.'

'Certainly.' I added the sweetener, then, milk steamed, poured a bit of that in as well.

'A little more, please?' She pivoted to Atherton, who was still waiting patiently for her latte.

Lest I overflow the cup, I dumped her drink into a latte mug, then added more milk.

'And a little foam?'

I reached for my long-handled spoon and dropped a dollop of foam on top. 'Anything else?'

The woman had already managed to wangle the equivalent of a latte—though, admittedly, made with brewed coffee instead of espresso—for the price of a black coffee. Maybe she'd like me to tap a vein, as well.

'Not a thing.' She put two dollars on the counter and carried her enhanced drink under her enhanced boobs to a table in the corner.

I took a tall glass, tore open another Splenda and poured the powder down the middle. Then I stirred in the espresso and added milk, topping off my creation with a couple of ice cubes.

'Perfect,' Atherton said, taking out a fiver. 'And keep the change, please.'

Gladly. I felt a chorus of 'She works hard for the money' coming on, a la Donna Summer. 'What can I get you today, MaryAnne?'

MaryAnne approached, studying the menu board as she came. 'I believe I'd like to try something new and exciting?' Despite the syrupy Southern accent, Mary-Anne still struck me as more down-to-earth than her Barbie friends. 'Any suggestions, Maggy?'

'Maybe our seasonal specialty drink?' I said, pointing. 'Triple Shot, fully-loaded.'

'Ah, for the days when *I* was fully loaded,' Mary-Anne said ruefully, glancing back at the women she was with. 'It made so many things—and people—so much more bearable.'

MaryAnne made no secret of the fact that she'd battled drug and alcohol addictions throughout a privileged adolescence in Atlanta where, according to her, neither parent—or anybody else—had ever told her 'no'.

MaryAnne moved here and eventually cowboyed up to 'just say no' herself, to both drugs and booze. And she'd never forgotten the people who'd helped. The alcohol treatment center on the east side of town bore her name as proudly as did the interior design firm she'd built on the foundation of her recovery.

'I'm afraid you'll have to deal, friends-wise,' I said. 'The "loaded" part is only sugar. Or I can make it Splenda, if you prefer.'

'Hell, no,' she said, Southern belle morphing into Southern broad. 'And use whole milk…'

She paused and we both looked skyward, as if waiting for lightning to strike.

Nothing.

MaryAnne shrugged. 'Well then, Maggy, let's really tempt fate and make it cream instead. I have very few vices left and I prefer to make the most of them.'

Like I said, a good shit, our MaryAnne.

'Where's Elaine today?' I asked, more because I was wondering what she'd told the other women than that I really cared. 'Isn't she part of your league?'

'Elaine? I'm afraid she doesn't play on Thursday, even in the club's round-robin. Because of Gabriella, you see.'

'Gabriella?' The woman in question had gotten a straw from the condiment cart and was settling into a chair across from… I'd forgotten her name already. 'What is your other friend's name?'

'The brunette? Why, Jane Smith.'

Yeah, like I'd remember that one. 'So, Gabriella and Elaine don't like each other?'

'It's more that Gabriella and Elaine's husband liked each other…better.'

I pictured my dentist ex-husband, Ted, with his hygienist. Same old song, in Brookhills, yet someone new was always humming along, thinking they'd composed it.

I snapped back to the moment. 'Making Elaine the "ex" that Gabriella mentioned?'

'Yes, poor thing. One morning she forgot her tennis racket and rushed home to get it? Robert and Gabriella were in his and Elaine's marital bed doing the tangled tango.'

A variation on the 'horizontal mambo', no doubt. At least my ex-husband had been considerate enough to do his hygienist off-campus. Though, come to think of it, in the dental chair I'd bought him.

'Did Elaine suspect?' I honestly hadn't. In retrospective, I probably should have, but…'You know, with Gabriella in the same tennis league and all?'

'Honey, that was the genius part. The two of them rotated? Elaine was our fourth on Monday, Tuesday and Wednesday, with Gabriella covering Thursday and Friday.'

'So when Elaine was playing on Monday…'

'Or Tuesday or Wednesday, Gabriella was playing on Robert. Or vice versa.' MaryAnne wasn't even bothering to keep her voice down.

'That's awful.' But, as MaryAnne had characterized the cloak-and-dagger cover story, also brilliant.

Except…'If Gabriella wasn't married herself, why didn't Robert just go to her place?'

'*She* says it was because people in the lovely, gated community where she lives would talk.'

'But you don't believe that?' Personally, I could see that a gate guard or neighbor might notice the same car, containing the same man, arriving each week.

MaryAnne shrugged. 'Our Gabriella likes to win. "Doing it" in Elaine's house, with Elaine's husband…'

'Proved she had.'

'As surely as if she were a male dog peeing on another's territory,' MaryAnne said.

That explained a lot of things, Frank-wise.

'And then there's the rush, of course.'

'Rush?' I repeated. 'As in, haste?' Given this group and their two-hour tennis matches, followed by leisurely coffee or even lunch, there should have been plenty of time for a 'quickie'. Or even a longie.

'No, honey.' MaryAnne permitted herself a small smile, probably at my naiveté. 'I'm talking about the adrenaline rush of the "game". I remember it very well from my days of playing hide-the-bottle.' Another smile, but this one self-deprecating. 'Or illegal substance. I swear,' MaryAnne continued, 'poor Elaine was an absolute wreck. She lost fifteen pounds and didn't have them to lose. When it first happened, I insisted she stay with me for a while and, after a week or so, I thought she'd turned the corner. Then she went home and the other Choo dropped.'

As in Jimmy Choo, the shoe designer. All I could do these days was visit the high-end shoes at Saks Fifth

Avenue, like I was touring a museum. Once a salesperson even let me touch one. 'The "other Choo" being?'

'Elaine got the house and the lion's share of their investments.'

'What's so terrible about that?' I'd have killed for a deal like that. Not literally, you understand.

'As it turns out, their house had a hefty mortgage on it to start with, then lost half its value in the housing crash. And the investments? Sunk into a Midwestern, Madoff-like Ponzi scheme.'

'And here I was feeling bad about not striking a deal like that with my ex. Though there were no investments to be had anyway. Just a used water pic.'

MaryAnne laughed, if a tad grimly. 'Strange as it sounds, Maggy, I've been on both sides of the money equation and I'd choose yours. You were able to keep your friends, but "ladies" like us—' she quirked one thumb at herself and the other toward the Barbie table— 'we'd drop you like a hot potato if your money ran out.'

'Maybe they would,' I said as I put her latte on the counter, 'but not you, MaryAnne.'

'I surely hope not.' She took the drink. 'Not to resurrect what can't be a pleasant topic for you, but I understand the body found under the platform was another real estate agent. One who worked for your partner?'

'I didn't know the sheriff had released her identity,' I said, glancing over at MaryAnne's table. 'Do they know?'

'I'm not sure what Gabriella and Jane might have heard, since we drove separately? I caught it on my car radio though the broadcast just gave the woman's name, not her affiliation.'

'Of course, I'd forgotten. You'd have known Brigid from showing your house.'

'I'd met her, certainly, but I was under the impression Sarah was taking care of everything, including my open house on Friday.'

I'd say that was a pretty safe bet now.

MaryAnne might be down-to-earth, but she still expected the boss to handle her listing personally. And who could blame her, especially when the only other option was an unlicensed apprentice?

'Well, that's neither here nor there,' MaryAnne continued. 'I did know Brigid, both from Kingston Realty and from Sapphire. I must say, though, that given the hours the girl kept there, I'd have been concerned about her being assigned to my affairs.'

MaryAnne had me nearer the beginning of her reply. 'You hang out at Sapphire?'

I didn't mean the question the way it came out, but MaryAnne laughed, not even a 'tad grimly' this time.

'Maggy, my dear. I may be sixty-five but I'm not dead?'

'You're sixty-five?' I gasped. 'Holy shit. I had you pegged fifteen years younger.'

'Thank you. It's the result of eating exactly what I want, exercising moderately and consulting an excellent foreign surgeon quarterly.'

To my eye, nary a tell-tale of lift nor tuck nor plump. 'As the woman at the next table said in *When Harry Met Sally*, "I'll have what she's having". And I can't see a trace of work.'

'That, my dear, is why she's excellent. I'll be happy

to give you her name when and if you should ever need it. Now, you were saying about Sapphire?'

I held up my hands, palms out. 'I have no standing because I've never been there, yet, but I had the impression it...'

'...is a meat market where only Kobe beef need apply? The glitzy ladder of perceived upward mobility? Ultimate mecca of the perennially self-absorbed? Guilty as charged. But, honey, what a moneymaker.'

'I was going to say "draws a younger crowd", but... wait a second. "Guilty as charged"? MaryAnne, do you *own* Sapphire?'

'Yes, of course, though with a partner? I was brought in to decorate the place and management couldn't pay the bill. The rest, as they say...' MaryAnne was staring out a platform-side window. 'Whatever do you suppose they're about to do?'

I turned in time to see a tow truck carrying a white Toyota rumble over the railroad tracks. 'Is that your car?'

'Of course not. I buy only American. I meant them.' She pointed.

Two people crossed in front of the far window. One had a pickaxe over his shoulder, the other a shovel. 'I have no clue.'

Pushing through the swinging service gate and crossing to the platform door, I hoped for some kind of public-works excavation. But, please God, not the exhumation of yet another body from an impromptu grave. What I hadn't expected was the coffeehouse equivalent of Caddyshack. 'There's a prairie-dog colony in our lawn.'

'Treasure hunters, more likely.' MaryAnne had followed me.

I stepped out onto the platform where I could see even more holes. Three on the grassy islands of the parking lot, several others yet closer to the building and along the sidewalk running up to the yellow police tape. 'The news coverage must have mentioned the money that supposedly went missing all those years ago.'

'And connected it to your hidden room. Did you know it existed?'

'MaryAnne, until yesterday, I knew nothing about our Mafia, their room or their loot.' Not to mention Sarah's problem with her apprentice, nor the fact Brigid Ferndale was dead.

Ignorance, I realized—and not for the first time— truly is bliss.

MaryAnne craned her neck to see around the corner. 'Interesting psychology, Maggy, don't you think? The logical place to prospect would be the room where Brigid was found, but the police have that taped off, so people are digging wherever else they can.'

There weren't enough psychiatrist's couches in Brookhills to analyze this particular brand of nutsiness. 'Do you remember exactly what the news reported?'

'I heard it on WTVR's FM radio affiliate?' MaryAnne said. 'They updated the discovery of the body by identifying the woman as Brigid Ferndale, and then segued into this special they're doing—*The Mystery of Romano's Raid*, or some such title.'

WTVR was the local television station where Kate had once worked and aspired to work again. The newspaper editor had probably given them an exclusive.

But…'Romano's Raid?' I repeated. Apparently 'The Brookhills' Massacre' had lost out, less to sensitivity and good taste and more to alliteration and brevity. 'Sounds like a Burt Lancaster movie.'

MaryAnne laughed, retracing her steps into the depot. 'Well, I'd best get back to our table. You hang in there, honey.'

'MaryAnne, wait.'

She turned.

'I'm planning to visit Sapphire tonight. Any chance you'd like to come with me?'

MaryAnne studied my face. 'You're going to Sapphire?'

'Hey, I'm…' I almost said twenty years younger than you, which—though true, would *not* have been advancing—'…not dead, either, you know.'

'You're a mere youngster, Maggy. But I was wondering, why Sapphire? Everyone who goes there wants something, whether it's a trophy wife, a rich husband, an investor, a new job or just plain strange.'

'Strange?'

'Strange stuff,' she explained. 'Though I don't think that's your style, especially with that lovely sheriff at your beck and call?'

Strange…ohhh, *stuff.* I got it. MaryAnne *did* have a way with words.

The owner of what she herself called a 'meat market' raised her eyebrows. 'So, if you're not looking to hook-up personally *or* professionally, information must be what you're after—more specifically, about Brigid. And you, my dear, think I can help?'

'I'm "guilty as charged", too,' I said. 'But you own

the place and—' I glanced over at her table where the two other women were still talking and beckoned Mary-Anne to join them—'I understand it may be the last place Brigid Ferndale was seen alive.'

After saying it so bluntly, I feared I'd overplayed my cards. MaryAnne was a business-owner. Given that, was it wise to tell her that a murder victim might have been offed after leaving her establishment?

Apparently so. MaryAnne's eyes flash-fired with excitement. 'Really?'

'Really.' I canted my head. 'But I can't say more now. Are we on?'

'Wouldn't miss it for…the…world! Shall we meet there at, say, eleven thirty?'

'*Eleven* thirty?' Bad enough the place didn't open until ten. Doesn't anybody else sleep? Or have to get up the next morning?

'It *is* a tad early?' she said. 'But on a Thursday night the crowd will be down, and I have a six a.m. spin class at my spa the next morning.'

I almost asked if she owned the spa, too.

MaryAnne had started for the table again and me, for the service area, when she spoke to my back. 'Oh, I'm sorry, Maggy, but one question?'

'Sure.' Turning toward her, I caught the swinging gate so it couldn't smack me in the butt.

'You have to know people are talking, right?' Again, she quirked a thumb toward her tablemates.

'Talking?'

MaryAnne moved back a step, then stage-whispered. 'For now, honey, they find you interesting. The acci-

dents, the body count, the—' finger-flicking air quotes—
'"investigations"?'

I didn't know what to say. So for a change, I kept silent.

MaryAnne continued, 'And, therefore, so long as any
related "inquiries" don't involve them or their friends
personally, your curiosity is just that—a curiosity. Even
a diversion?'

A diversion. From what? Leading their lives of glitzy
desperation? 'By them, I assume you mean Brookhills'
elite?'

'Or those who consider themselves to be such?' She
held up her hands. 'For my part, I think you're a…do
you know what a mensch is? It's a Yiddish expression.'

Yiddish. From our *numero uno* Southern belle?

'An unrepentant, overly officious intermeddler?' It
was how Pavlik described me, so I figured it was as
good a guess as any.

A grin crinkled the area around MaryAnne's eyes.
No Botox there. 'I'm sure you're that, too, honey, but
no. A mensch means, literally, a human being…'

So far, so good.

'…but it's come to mean someone with honor and in-
tegrity. Someone you'd be happy to spend time with. A
guy—or gal—who wants the best for the people around
her, and will stand up to secure it.'

I felt vaguely uncomfortable, having pretty much
lived my life under the banner of 'under-promise and
over-deliver'. And sometimes even that set my bar too
high. Mensch-dom seemed far out of reach.

'MaryAnne, you give me too much credit. Essentially, I'm selfish and self-involved. I can't even remem-

ber—' I waved vaguely at her table—'customers from visit to visit. I'm considering sticking name tags on their foreheads as I greet them at the door.'

The crinkling got deeper. 'Which begs my question, Maggy: if you, like Rhett Butler, truly don't give a damn, why do you continue to be an "unrepentant, overly officious intermeddler"?'

I looked around the coffeehouse. The tables that needed to be wiped. The coffee that needed to be ground. The Barbies, who were just plain...needy.

A shrug. 'I get bored?'

ELEVEN

'I LIKE YOUR STYLE, Maggy Thorsen,' MaryAnne Williams said. 'Always have.'

'Same here. See you tonight?'

'As I said, I wouldn't miss it.' MaryAnne moved on to her table and I got on with the myriad chores I'd let slide as I sat with my tablet of paper, making lists of how to find out why Brigid had died instead of doing what I should have been.

MaryAnne could think I was being modest, but there was a lot of truth in what I'd said.

I *did* get bored, dammit. I loved planning the coffeehouse. I loved *opening* the coffeehouse, and even its *re*-opening. But...working there? Not so much.

I picked up a damp rag and crossed to a crumb-covered, coffee-ringed table to wipe it down for the next hungry, thirsty slobs.

Who were, in turn, *my* bread and butter.

And it's not that I manufactured the crimes and bodies to escape the mundane. They just seemed to drop into my lap. Or, in the case of Brigid Ferndale, my subterranean room.

And as for the 'intermeddling', if I was able to help the people involved, well...that made *me* happy.

And wasn't that, when you boiled it all down, selfishness? Me, a mensch? I didn't think so.

The chimes on the street-side door jingled and I glanced up from the table I'd been wiping—and wiping and wiping—as I'd been thinking.

A man with a buzz-cut and a muscular physique, but wearing a business suit and topcoat, stepped across our threshold and looked around.

'Robert,' Gabriella Atherton called. 'Over here.'

He turned and caught sight of the ladies who do lunch—and occasionally other women's husbands—at their corner table.

'Hello, sweetheart,' he said, leaning down to kiss the top of Atherton's head.

Robert. Of course, this was Elaine Riordan's ex-husband, now Gabriella Atherton's fiancé. Who dared imply that Maggy Thorsen couldn't remember names?

Oh, yeah. That would be me.

I approached their table, telling myself I was being a good server, but knowing the nosy truth in my despicable heart of hearts. 'Can I get you anything? Or, everybody else, refills?'

'Oh, that would be fabulous,' Atherton said for both her and… Jan… Jane?—yes, that was it—pushing their cups toward me.

Robert said, 'No, thanks. I can't stay.' Then to Atherton: 'I just saw your car and wanted to stop by, say hello. I'm on my way to the courthouse.'

A cellphone blinged the abbreviated signal that indicates a text message and three of the people went digging. Gabriella Atherton and Jane Smith into their purses, Robert Riordan into his suit jacket pocket.

MaryAnne Williams looked on with the pitying—nay, withering—smile of the non-addicted.

Robert said, 'Mine,' as though he'd won a coveted, if somehow shady, lottery. He punched one button and then, rather abruptly, a second before plunging the phone back into his pocket. 'Not important.'

Right.

Gabriella Atherton wasn't fooled either. 'Who was it?'

'Just Elaine—' he waved his hand a little too nonchalantly—'with another question about COBRA.'

'Cobra? I thought that was a rattlesnake,' Smith said.

Everyone looked at her.

'I mean your Marine tattoo, Robert. You know, "Don't tread on me"?'

Ahh, I got it. Didn't understand it, but…

'Jane, how did you happen to see—' Atherton started to say.

'COBRA is an acronym,' I hastily injected by way of conciliatory interruption. The last thing I needed today was a coffeehouse cat fight. 'C… O… B… R… A with all capital letters.'

Smith threw me a startled, who-asked-you look. And here I was just trying to help bail her out of an embarrassing—if obviously unappreciated—situation.

Maybe MaryAnne Williams was right. I really *was* a mensch.

Though no good deed goes unpunished.

'COBRA stands for the Consolidated Omnibus Budget Reconciliation Act,' I drove bravely onward. 'It allows people to extend health-insurance coverage through their former employers' plans. If you can afford it.'

Another lesson learned from personal experience.

Both an individual health-insurance plan and, now, a group plan for our small business, had each proved cheaper than using COBRA after the divorce.

'Or your former husband's insurance plan, in this case.' Atherton nodded to Robert. 'Go ahead and get back to her, if you need to.' She chin-gestured toward his pocket, looking all the world like the perfect future wife, totally unconcerned about any residual gravitational pull Robert might feel from his former spouse's orbit.

'Thanks, Gabriella. And I will, though I don't know why she's asking. Elaine dropped her COBRA months ago.' He gave Atherton a kiss on the cheek. 'I appreciate your understanding.'

'Hey,' Atherton said, waving her hand. 'I know what it's like to be there.' A smile, though sickly sweet. 'I'm just glad this realtor doesn't have to be anymore. On *my* own, I mean.'

The woman looked up at her fiancé with obvious affection. Barbie in love with GI Joe. Go figure.

It was nearly seven when I turned the deadbolt on the front door of Uncommon Grounds, and then let myself out its platform one. Securing that deadbolt, too, I realized the palm of my right hand was itching.

'You'll be getting money soon,' I could hear my grandmother saying in my head.

'That would be very welcome, Grandma,' I replied out loud as I descended the steps toward the depot's parking lot. 'I could use it to fix our Swiss-cheesed lawn.'

Not wanting to bother Pavlik's overburdened sheriff's department, I'd called the town police and they had been kind enough to send an officer by to shoo away the treasure hunters. The holes, though, remained, which I realized as I veered off the sidewalk toward my car and nearly twisted an ankle.

But…hole? It seemed more like someone had been laying pipe, parallel to the sidewalk and about three feet inside of it. Or maybe they had, back in the day, and I'd just never noticed the topographical dip. After all, the wastewater from the toilet and sink in the waiting room had to be borne away somewhere.

Driving my Escape home, I tried to figure out what I should wear that night. It'd been a *looong* time since I'd gone clubbing in Brookhills.

Try, like never.

A small, 'bachelorette' apartment on the East Side of Milwaukee had been my home when I was single. It was only after Ted and I married that we'd moved to Brookhills and by that time my 'clubbing' days were over, fondly remembered through a haze of Bartles and Jaymes wine coolers.

So, proper attire for Sapphire? I had no idea, but figured 'twas better to err on the conservative side. Maybe a nice skirt with a pretty cami and a jacket I could take off if I felt too buttoned up.

Perfect, I thought, as I walked toward my house's front door. This way I won't look like I'm trying too hard. Or trying at all, for that matter.

I went through the usual act with Frank, who apparently had gotten over his snit enough to shove past me toward bolting to the nearest tree, then follow me into our kitchen for his treat.

From there, I went straight to the laundry room, where I stripped off my jeans and Uncommon Grounds T-shirt and then on to the bathroom and its shower. When the hot water hit me, a kaleidoscopic scent of coffee beans arose. While at work, the stuff seemed to sink into your pores. And while coffee is a relatively positive smell—enticing even—you don't necessarily want to become one with it 24/7/365.

I shampooed once and realized my right palm was still itching. Also red, though that may have been due to the hot water or the scratching I'd done earlier. I stuck my hand out past the shower curtain into the better light of an overhead fixture to get a better look.

And that's when I heard something. 'Frank?'

No answer.

'Frank, is that you?'

A partial bark answered me, but like the sheepdog had been somehow quieted.

Uh-oh.

I shut off the water, not bothering to finish rinsing my hair. Janet Leigh might have been perfectly clean on the floor of that Bates Motel shower, but what good did it do her? Or her sheepdog.

Stepping over the side of my tub, I pulled a green flowered towel off the rack and wrapped it around me. A squeak now, from outside the bathroom door but certainly inside my bedroom. Floorboard perhaps? Or bedspring? Whatever, but Frank didn't squeak. The big lummox thudded. Bounded.

Or, when he was feeling stealthy, he padded.

But Frank never squeaked.

'Jake, you…' I tried to say conversationally, but it

didn't come out. Clearing my throat, I started again. 'You must hear that, too. Get your gun out of the...' Where in the hell would my supposed shower-mate have stashed a gun in *this* room? '...um, the linen closet, Jake.'

Another squeak, this one seeming startled, assuming noises can be startled.

'I'll open the door,' I continued loudly. 'And you just start shooting. OK, Sheriff Pavlik?'

'OK,' from the other side of the door.

I cracked it open. 'Pavlik?'

Sure enough. The sheriff got up from the foot of my bed, just as Frank came romping toward him, tennis ball in the pooch's slobbery mouth.

I was incredibly relieved. And, therefore, pissed. 'How did you get in?'

'Your door was ajar and I was worried,' he said, looking me and my towel up and down. 'Even more so, when I heard you talking like somebody was next to you in the shower.'

'You were supposed to be scared away. By *you*.'

'Well, since I knew it wasn't me...' Pavlik pushed open the door and my towel slipped.

I grabbed the cotton hem. 'Yeah?'

'Oh, yeah.' He ran his hand up my bare arm and across its shoulder as he dropped his lips to the notch below my throat.

As Pavlik kissed me there and worked his way southward, I felt my towel fall away completely. He murmured, 'You know how I knew it wasn't me in there with you?'

'N...n...no!' Apparently I'd suddenly developed a

stutter. Then my back arched on its own and I tangled my fingers in Pavlik's dark, curly hair.

He craned his head back to look up at me. 'Maggy, you *never* call me Jake.'

TURNS OUT THAT eleven thirty wasn't all that late. In fact, after Pavlik left I had time for only a quick turn-around shower.

I hadn't told our sheriff about my visit to Sapphire, lest he think I was officiously intermeddling. Besides, it felt a little like cheating. Not that I planned to. Cheat, that is. Officious intermeddling, however, was quite definitely in my plans.

I'd briefly considered scolding Pavlik for showing up at my house unannounced and then letting himself in. But…a tremor at the memory, it had been an awfully nice surprise.

Exercising uncharacteristic decisiveness at home—I'd decided to stay the conservative course on dress-code and therefore mirror-front dithering was kept to a minimum—I pulled up in front of Sapphire only a minute or two past half past eleven. By day, you wouldn't even know the place was there. Or, if you did notice the empty parking lot and hulking building with its windows blocked out on the edge of an industrial park, you'd think it was just another vacant warehouse.

But at night? My-oh-my, things were *très différent*.

The parking lot was packed and after joining the parade of cars looking for spaces, I gave in and circled back to the building, waiting this time for the luxury of paying the valet fifteen bucks to park my Escape.

Leaving my keys and my vehicle, I hurried to the

canopied door, where I was stopped by a man with a clipboard.

'Name?'

'Maggy Thorsen, but I don't think I'd be on—'

'Go right in, Ms Thorsen.' He unclipped a velvet rope just like you see on television and a muscular young man opened the door for me, giving me an almost quizzical once-over as I passed by.

When I stepped through the entrance, I realized why.

'Toto, we're not in Kansas anymore,' I said under my breath.

The foyer was huge, with a vacated hostess stand to one side. The only light came, faintly, from sconces on the dark walls. Although, no more illumination really was needed. Young women, in short dresses layered in sequins and spangles of various types, were everywhere. Female walking/talking mirror balls, most of them heading to or from the restroom. Though why any bothered was a mystery to me. They all seemed to be grooming on the fly. Applying lip gloss, tidying their hair. I even saw one woman pulling a set of tweezers out of a tiny clutch bag. I wondered what kind of plucking emergency had sent her scurrying from the dance floor.

Where the foyer and bathroom brigade had contained mostly women, inside there seemed to be a more even ratio of men to women. If spangly dresses were *de rigueur* for women, the men of Sapphire seemed to have, for once, more options. Suits drew even with sports jackets. Just a nice pair of slacks, dress shirt open at the neck and sleeves rolled up seemed comfortably in the competition.

Some clubbers were already pairing off, but others

ranged in packs, drinks in hand, surveying the crowd. Still early, I thought. Plenty of time to rove individually, cut someone of the opposite sex—or same sex, as the case might be—off from the herd and engage them for a minute, an hour or even a lifetime.

By 1 a.m., I wagered, the now-nearly vacant dance floor would be pulsing with people. Some moving with the percussion of the pumped-up house music, others dancing to the beat of their hearts.

Or, let's face it, wallets and purses.

I slowly did a three-sixty, trying to get my bearings. In fact, *any* bearing, singular. The walls and ceiling were nearly completely covered with mirrored glass panels, the tables surrounding the dance floor seeming to march on to infinity. Left of the entry...

'Hey, honey,' a voice said.

No, not the man of my dreams.

I turned to see MaryAnne Williams, who was wearing a long-sleeved version of the requisite spangly number.

I was *seriously* underdressed.

Well, no matter. I was there to work. 'Hi, Mary-Anne—' giving her a hug—'I was running late, so I didn't have time to change.'

A small fib, but one I hoped could be first accepted, then forgiven. If my funeral plan called for burning in hell, I figured that far worse transgressions were already ledgered into His Big Book of Sins under my name.

'You're not at all late, Maggy, and you look wonderful.'

When you normally saw somebody in jeans and a T-shirt, I guessed pretty much anything was an improvement.

'Can I get you a drink?' she asked, motioning me

toward a bar stool. 'I had a chance to ask around and I think you'll be interested in what folks told me.'

'About Brigid?'

'And more.'

'Evening, ladies.' A bartender with red curly hair and freckles put cocktail napkins in front of us.

'I'll have a tonic and lime, Benjy,' MaryAnne said. 'Oh, and this is the woman I was telling you about?'

'Maggy Thorsen,' I said, extending my hand to shake his.

'A pleasure.' Benjy reciprocating. 'What can I get you?'

'Red wine?'

He slid a laminated twelve-inch long menu card to me.

'Oh, I don't need this,' I said, sliding the 'wine list' back toward him. 'Whatever you have by the glass.'

A faint smile from Benjy. 'But, ma'am, these *are* what we offer by the glass.'

'All of…?' There had to be twenty-five different entries, many with prices I could easily have mistaken for by-the-bottle tags.

'Maggy, Sapphire has a wonderful wine selection,' MaryAnne said. 'Benjy, show her the full wine list.'

The artifact he held up looked like a leather-bound Manhattan telephone directory. 'Would you like to look?'

'Uh, no. Thanks,' I said, and read off the cheapest red atop the by-the-glass offering.

'You don't want that Pinot, Maggy. It's dreck. Benjy, bring her a glass of the Cakebread Cab,' MaryAnne commanded, sounding more savvy club-owner than Southern belle.

'Will do, Ms Williams.'

'I love red wine,' I told MaryAnne as her bartender slid a balloon-bowl glass from the overhead rack, 'but I'm afraid if I don't recognize a bottle from the shelves of my grocery store, I'm lost.'

OK, maybe an exaggeration, but I figured it was an acceptable—even slick—way of reminding MaryAnne that my wallet was considerably thinner than hers. If I wasn't mistaken, the wine she'd ordered for me was listed at twenty dollars. American. Per glass, plus tax and tip.

'Not to worry, my dear. You will *really* enjoy this wine, I think, and it's my treat. Despite the fact I don't drink it anymore, I love wine and I've taken great pride in layering Sapphire's wine cellar.'

Benjy returned with the big glass, about an inch of a lovely wine between red and purple in color glowing in the light from the pendant fixtures also suspended above the bar. 'Before Ms Williams took over the wine-buying, people would ask what wines we had, and I'd have to recite, deadpan, "red, white and blush". And then blush myself.'

I laughed and took the glass he'd set in front of me. I swirled its contents as Benjy filled a rocks glass with ice, tonic and a freshly cut wedge of lime for MaryAnne.

'Go ahead,' she said. 'Try it.'

And so I did. Carefully. At twenty bucks the inch, I wasn't about to chug this puppy. And the vintage was, admittedly, heaven come to earth. I'd definitely not be finding this wine on the shelves of Pick 'n Save during my lifetime, and probably not during that of my son, Eric.

'Taste the black fruit?' MaryAnne asked eagerly. 'And there should be some roasted coffee and dark chocolate tones, as well.'

Danged if she wasn't right. 'I do. And…and—' I sniffed the wine—'caramel?'

'Bravo,' she said, taking a sip of her tonic water. 'Your good palate deserves better than grocery-store stock, though I have to say there are some very drinkable wines available for under ten dollars the bottle.'

But those weren't wine/coffee/dessert melded seamlessly in one lovely mouthful. I set down the glass so I wouldn't guzzle its remaining contents. 'MaryAnne, I know you've quit drinking. Does that include wine?'

'Sadly, my dear, yes. Alcohol, by any other name, is still alcohol. At least in my case.'

'So how can you know the way this—' I nail-tapped my own glass and it gave off a regal ping—'tastes?'

'I read, study. And I supplement that information with opinions from people like you, who have a palate and a nose. Not, by the way, the same gauges. For example, many won't be able to detect those caramel notes.'

'Well, any time you want an opinion,' I said, taking another seductive but cautious sip, 'I'm your woman.'

I set the glass down, suddenly feeling guilty about deriving such pleasure from something MaryAnne obviously loved, but couldn't touch. 'Isn't it difficult, though, being around wine—even studying it, as you say—when you can't partake yourself?'

'Strangely, Maggy? No. I'd describe it as cooking my family a great dinner when I'm dieting. You are enjoying the wine, which validates my decision to buy that one and place it prominently on Sapphire's list in the first place. And choose it for you, in particular. It keeps me…' She seemed to be searching for a word.

'In the game?'

'Exactly.' MaryAnne beamed at me and resettled on her stool. 'I imagine it's not much different from your desire to find out how and why Brigid Ferndale ended up in such an undignified state at your place of business. Your need to feel in control of your destiny. In the game, as you say, even if it's more your sheriff's baili-wick than your own.'

I hated to think what Pavlik would say about mur-der investigation as sport, though Sherlock Holmes certainly viewed it that way, with his 'Come, Watson, come! The game is afoot'.

But then, Holmes was a fictional character.

I swirled some more Cakebread Cab. 'Did you say you'd found out who Brigid was with on Monday night?'

'I did.' MaryAnne nodded toward the bartender, who was washing out glasses. 'Benjy saw them.'

'Really?' Wow, interrogating employees was easy when the boss sat next to you and subpoenaed the wit-ness.

MaryAnne said to Benjy, 'I told Ms Thorsen that you'd seen Brigid Ferndale on Monday night.'

'That's right.'

'What time was she here?' I asked.

'I checked when the sheriff's deputies questioned me.' He closed his eyes. 'Ms Ferndale opened her tab at eleven ten and settled up at…uhm, twenty minutes past midnight.'

No surprise that Pavlik's people had already been here, asking the same questions I was. The negligible difference might be that I was familiar with the Brookhills community, though—glancing at the milling mass of spike-heeled lasses and hair-restored lads—not *this* aspect of it.

'An hour and ten minutes, then?' I asked Benjy. 'That doesn't seem very long.' Unless Brigid had met someone. And left with him. Or her.

'It's not, for Bri—' a sideways cut toward Mary-Anne—'for Ms Ferndale. Most nights she'd clock in around eleven and stay 'til last call.'

Well, I suppose Sarah's apprentice could always come in late or sleep at the Kingston Realty office the next day. After all, who'd be there to know? But...

'Did you say "clock in"?' The phrase made me wonder if Brigid mightn't have had a second job.

In the 'hospitality' industry's oldest profession.

'Just a figure of speech,' Benjy said, proving he really *could* blush. 'Brigid would always stop by the bar when she arrived, order a drink and leave her purse with me.'

'Her purse?' There was an edge of displeasure in MaryAnne's voice. 'Benjy, you open a tab with just a charge card, *not* the whole handbag. What if her wallet had disappeared and she claimed you'd stolen it? The club—*my* club—could be liable.'

Now Benjy was bright red. 'Brig... Ms Ferndale wouldn't do that.'

'So says you,' MaryAnne snapped. 'Edict, from this moment to the end of the world: you do *not* store customers' personal items behind my bar, do you understand?'

'Yes'm.' The bartender looked miserable. Yet another nice, young man duped by a conniving pretty woman.

I cleared my throat. 'Benjy, did Brigid meet someone here Monday night?'

'Well, like I told Ms Williams and the deputies, Ms Ferndale tended to wander. That's why she didn't want to carry...' Benjy glanced at MaryAnne and left it at that.

'When you say "wander"...?'

'We called it cruising in my day,' MaryAnne said. 'Working the room.'

And with no visible handbag, Brigid probably got showered with free drinks by all hopefuls for the duration. Shrewd of her.

'Did you see who she might have wandered to?' I asked.

'Well, that's the odd part. Monday night, Ms Ferndale stayed close to the bar here. Said she was meeting someone later. I knew she'd been looking for a new job, because she hated the wom—' another glance at MaryAnne—'the one she had.'

Even I would have to concede that Sarah Kingston was, at best, an acquired taste. 'So you had the impression the person Brigid was waiting for was going to offer her a job?'

Benjy frowned. 'I don't know that. She didn't seem to be sure. Something about her needing to be a...rainmaker?'

'Meaning bring in new clients,' MaryAnne said. 'That explains why Brigid would bad-mouth Sarah when I'd call. That little snake in the grass wanted to hijack me from Kingston Realty and carry my house listing along to a new firm.'

'Were you going to jump ship?' I asked.

'Are you kidding?' MaryAnne snorted. 'Brigid spent three or four hours a night minimum in this club alone. Do you think I'd trust Ms Swinging Disco with the sale of my two-million-dollar home?'

The mental reactions of Maggy Thorsen, in the order they overwhelmed her:

Holy shit. Two million dollars?

And then: *MaryAnne, given the amount of time Sarah had spent at Kingston Realty lately, you already were trusting Brigid with selling your home. You just didn't know it.*

I said, 'OK, Benjy. What time did this person Brigid was waiting for show up?'

He shook his head. 'Sorry, but it was busy for a Monday, so I had other customers to serve.'

'And pretty girls' handbags to mind?' From Mary-Anne.

I prompted Benjy. 'So, Brigid came in a little after eleven…'

'And about fifteen, twenty minutes later, a woman came in and asked for Brigid, so I pointed her out.'

Hadn't he just said he'd been too busy to notice? 'What did this new woman look like?'

Benjy shrugged. 'Blonde hair, very slim.'

Without really needing to, I looked around. His description captured half the women currently in Sapphire. 'Dressed like all the…regulars?' I pointed to the dance floor which was now filling up.

'Not even close. This woman was wearing jeans.'

'You let people in jeans through the velvet rope?' I asked MaryAnne.

She shrugged and pointed to a woman in her early twenties crossing the room in skinny jeans, an off-the-shoulder cream-colored top, and the aura of original sin. 'Honey, those go for a thousand dollars the pair. Makes it kind of hard to diss them.'

Bet my mom-jeans would be 'dissed' plenty. 'So, the two of them spoke?'

'Yes. It seemed to me like they'd already met, but didn't really know each other, if you know what I mean?' Benjy glanced nervously at MaryAnne.

I could guess what he was thinking. The more information Benjy gave me, the less it would seem her bartender had been doing his job that night.

I turned to MaryAnne and whispered. Her eyes narrowed, but she appeared to understand. 'OK, Maggy, I'm going to do some paperwork. Benjy, call me in the office if she—or you—need anything.'

I gave her a hug. 'MaryAnne, thanks so much.'

'I expect to hear every word he has to tell you,' she murmured in my ear.

'Deal,' I whispered back. 'But only if you promise me that you won't fire him.'

A hesitation. Our clinch was getting a little long for comfort, though I wasn't sure in a place like Sapphire anyone would notice. Either they were in their own clinches or negotiating a deal toward doing so.

'Fine.' She let me go and I watched her leave. No wonder I liked the woman. MaryAnne was Sarah, but with money and charm, instead of piss and vinegar.

But, back to grilling Benjy. I took a sip of wine.

He motioned toward my glass. 'Ms Thorsen, can I freshen that for you?'

The tide *was* inexorably ebbing in the balloon-bowl, but given the price, I hesitated.

Benjy looked toward MaryAnne's path of departure then back to me with a conspiratorial smile. 'On the house. For covering my back just now with the boss.'

No need to hit me in the head with a hammer. Bartenders working for a place like this, I knew, were allowed a certain number of 'comps'—drinks they could 'buy' their good customers—per night. 'Thank you, Benjy.'

He poured me a bit more than an additional inch this time, and I asked him, 'Could you hear the two women's conversation?'

Benjy scrunched his facial features, then returned to 'normal' as I'd seen it on him. 'Something about showing a property, I think. They talked maybe thirty minutes and just before the other woman left, Brigid asked me for a piece of paper so she could write down a lockbox combination.'

A lockbox—sort of a mini safe—was affixed to the doorknob of a property that was on the market and contained the key for that listing's front door. It might seem a security risk, akin to putting a key under the welcome mat, but if a stranger doesn't know the combination, he or she can't open the lockbox and access the key. Accordingly, the system allowed an owner to provide a listing agency with only one key but still allow any associate who had an interested buyer to use the combination, get the key and show the house.

Presumably, Kingston Realty had lockboxes on a

number of residential and even commercial properties. But which particular one was this? MaryAnne's was likely the most valuable of the Kingston Realty listings.

I didn't like the idea of Brigid Ferndale essentially handing a key to MaryAnne's—or anyone else's—house to someone who wasn't in Sarah's firm.

And, since there were no other agents in Sarah's firm, who was…? 'Benjy, you're sure this woman was a blonde?'

I was thinking Gabriella Atherton, of course. A redhead.

Another conspiratorial smile from the bartender to the stars. 'Ms Thorsen, the lighting in Sapphire is set on "kind", but there are just so many blondes, you notice more the ones who aren't.'

I had another thought. Elaine Riordan was blonde and a real estate agent, dilettante or not. 'Was this other woman really thin? I mean, borderline emaciated?'

Benjy closed his eyes again. 'When this lady took off her coat, she seemed more athletic-skinny than diet-skinny like the women around here. Especially the older ones.'

I appreciated his candor, but…'Coat? On Monday night, the temperature was still in the sixties.'

And considered nippy, perhaps, for Florida, but Wisconsin? In October? People had been wearing shorts and flip-flops on Monday, but this woman wore a coat. Blonde, athletic-thin and a freezy-cat. The description fit Deirdre Doty to a tee.

'Did you tell the sheriff's deputy about this woman speaking to Brigid?'

Benjy was stacking glasses. 'I said she'd been talking to some people, but he didn't seem to think it was all that important.'

Because 'he' didn't know Brookhills and quasi-human nature the way I did.

My pulse quickened. 'Did you see Brigid Ferndale leave with this woman?'

'Nope, because Brigid had a second meeting.' He head-gestured toward the dance floor. 'With her.'

I scanned the crowd. 'Which her?'

'The redhead.'

The redhead. Somebody needed to give this kid a lesson in the clarity produced by linear storytelling.

I turned back to him. 'You mean there also was a redhead here Monday night?'

'Yeah, I told you. After the other woman left, Brigid hung out to meet with that chick who owns the real estate company.'

This time I followed his finger.

To Gabriella Atherton, gyrating without an apparent care in the middle of Sapphire's dance floor.

TWELVE

NOT REALLY A SURPRISE, I thought, as the current, unidentifiable song ended, and Gabriella Atherton disappeared into a crush on the far side of the floor.

We knew Brigid Ferndale wanted to work for Atherton. Upon further questioning, Benjy told me that after the first woman—presumably TV producer Deirdre Doty—left, Brigid went into the entrance foyer and returned with Atherton. The two had retired to a table and, not twenty minutes after sitting down, Brigid had paid her tab for the one drink she'd actually ordered, collected her handbag and left.

With Gabriella Atherton? Benjy hadn't noticed.

So, was Atherton the last person to see Brigid alive? That I didn't know.

But Atherton ought to be able to provide a few pieces to the puzzle.

I wended my way through the growing crowd on the dance floor and then started circling the far tables, searching for her. The strap of my purse was over my left shoulder, with the body of the bag tucked under that elbow. I held my wine glass out front in the opposite hand. My strategy was to protect the purse from pickpockets and my Cakebread Cabernet Sauvignon from the bag, lest it be sent swinging as I squeezed past clumps of seated people.

I probably looked like a punt-returner securing the football as I dodged the other patrons in a slow-motion, broken-field run.

'Maggy?'

I turned to see Ward Chitown and Deirdre Doty sitting at a table I'd overlooked.

'Would you care to join us?'

I didn't see why not. Maybe Doty could tell me something more. Like confirming what time she'd left Brigid Ferndale and why the sales apprentice had given the TV producer a lockbox combination.

'I'd love to, thanks.' I chose the chair next to Chitown and set down my glass.

'You're nearly empty, can I get you another?'

I looked at the tiny pool of wine number two in the bottom of its glass. Huh. 'That would be very nice, but it's the Cakebread Cab.'

Chitown blinked. 'However, you are enjoying it, correct?'

'Ward, enjoying it just doesn't capture the magic.'

Chitown nodded, waved over a waiter and placed the order for my drink, as well as two boutique bourbons—his straight up with a water chaser and Deirdre's on the rocks. I knew the bourbons would vie with the price of my wine because while he prefaced his and Deirdre's request with the word 'bourbon', I'd never heard of the distillery or the name of the whiskey itself.

Deirdre leaned forward over the table. 'I'm so glad we ran into you, Maggy. I really need someone—'

'Wait, wait,' Chitown interrupted. 'First things, first. Maggy, we would love for you to come to the show on Saturday. We think there's plenty of room at both the Ristorante and slaughterhouse for us to create a small—' an index finger went up—'and I do mean *small*, studio audience.'

'Including Elaine Riordan?' I asked.

'A very enthusiastic Elaine Riordan, who will be here any minute. Elaine will have her own moment in the sun,' Chitown said, 'as, happily, Deirdre's been able to put her to work.'

'I have to admit, the woman's a great source of information,' Doty said. 'Not only does she know everything you'd ever want to know—and more—about your town's history but also who's who and what's what in modern-day Brookhills. Elaine's the one who suggested I talk—'

But Chitown interrupted. Again. 'And, Maggy, we'd also like you to be part of our post-production celebration Saturday night here at Sapphire.'

'Sounds wonderful. I'd love to attend.'

'And bring your business partner, too. Sarah, is it?'

'Yes. I'll tell her.' I turned to Deirdre Doty. 'OK, now that your boss has buttered me up like a cob of summer sweetcorn, how can I help the cause?'

Doty laughed. 'He's always one to open with the good news, but in this case I hope that your helping us will help you as well. Two things: first, if the police have released the waiting room under the loading platform, would you allow us to film a backstory package in there to show on the program?'

'Have you spoken to the sheriff?' I asked.

'Not yet. I wanted to get your permission first.'

'That really would be up to Sarah, since she owns

not just our shop, but the entire depot. But so long as Pavlik says yes, then I guess—'

'Wonderful.' Doty pulled a notebook from the side pocket of her coat, which was hanging over the back of her chair. Apparently the long-sleeve cable-knit sweater she had on kept her warm enough to chance taking off the heavier outer layer.

Doty scribbled a few words. 'Second,' she continued, 'I need a caterer to provide a meal for the crew and guests on Saturday.'

'We're on a bit of a shoestring budget,' Chitown put in, 'but, if you're willing, we could pay for your out-of-pockets and give you mentions on the show and in the credits.'

'Product placement?' I asked. 'Coffee mugs with our Uncommon Grounds logo everywhere?'

'Just so we don't find them buried atop the treasure,' Doty said with a grin.

'That *would* be tacky.' I was getting excited about their idea. 'How about this? I'll talk to the woman who handles the food side of our operation tomorrow and see what she thinks. How many people are you talking about?'

'We're still working on that,' Doty said. 'Elaine is pulling together a local crew list and also a guest one. Can I have her call you tomorrow?'

'Why don't you have her call Tien directly? That way, they can work out details without us mucking up the middle.'

'Good idea.' Doty waited until the waiter, who'd returned with our drinks, set them before us, and then turned to a fresh page in her notebook. 'And this is Tien...?'

I took a sip of my wine. 'Romano.'

Ward Chitown looked up sharply. 'Romano? R... O... M... A... N... O? As in the Ristorante?'

Oh-oh. I looked at my glass of beguiling Cab. Traitorous grape. 'Ristorante? Gee, I don't know. I guess it could be a coincidence, but you should ask Tien.' Then, in hopes of a diversion and perhaps even catching the two by surprise: 'Speaking of coincidence, I understand you knew Brigid Ferndale?'

Chitown, for one, seemed confused by the change of subject. 'Brigid Ferndale?' He looked at Deirdre.

'That's the real estate agent for the Ristorante,' she said. 'You remember.'

'Oh, of course. The lovely young blonde.' Now to me. 'Brigid was kind enough to meet Deirdre on very short notice so we could get access to the property.' Then back to his producer. 'Did you invite her to the show, as well? I certainly think this Ms Ferndale has earned it.'

Aim right between the eyes. 'I'm sorry to say that you can't invite Ms Ferndale to anything. She's dead.' I gave it a beat. 'Haven't you seen the news?'

'No,' Doty said, her face staring at the tabletop, and her tone hollow. 'We've been in the Ristorante and the slaughterhouse all day, blocking the scenes. Wait a...' Now her head jerked up, and a hand went to her mouth. 'Don't tell me the body found in the waiting room was...'

'Brigid Ferndale.'

'Oh, dear.' Chitown took a mighty slug of his bourbon. 'That's awful.'

'I don't understand,' Deirdre said, looking to and fro between her boss and me. 'Ward, I thought *you* discovered the body. You had to have recognized her.'

Ahh. Chitown was telling his faithful followers *he'd* discovered the body? Not that I minded so much. God knows, Sarah and I had stumbled over more than our share.

Chitown swallowed. 'Well, Deirdre, I may have uh… ambiguously stated exactly what—'

'Ward didn't go all the way into the room where the body lay,' I told her. 'Probably all he saw were her legs. Right, Ward?'

'Right,' he said, favoring me with a full-voltage smile charged with charm and not just a little gratitude. 'Then Maggy asked me to step out and direct the authorities when they arrived.'

'But—'

'Am I interrupting?'

The voice of Sheriff Jake Pavlik came from above and behind my right shoulder. I twisted to gauge his mood, given I'd neglected to tell him I was going 'clubbing' after he'd left me tonight.

His eyes told me nothing, but he wore the same jeans and dress shirt he'd had on earlier. Over that— my heart be still and our cold spell be blessed—his buttery leather jacket.

I involuntarily reached out and stroked it, just managing to restrain a moan. That jacket and I had a beautiful thing going.

'Not at all.' Ward Chitown stood up. 'Sheriff Pavlik, correct?'

'Yes.' The two men shook hands, if not as prospective best friends.

'And I assume you know Maggy Thorsen?' Chitown had a safe bet there, given that I'd just fondled the sheriff's outerwear.

'Of course,' Pavlik said, nodding to me.

'Sheriff.'

Now Pavlik extended his hand to Deirdre. 'I'm sorry, but I don't think *we've* met. I'm Jake Pavlik.'

'Deirdre Doty. I'm Ward's show producer.' She motioned to the table next to us. 'I don't think they're using that chair if you'd like to join us?'

'Thanks.' Both Deirdre and I inch-humped our chairs sideways so Pavlik could pull his between us.

I asked, 'Sheriff, are you here on business or pleasure?'

'I could ask you the same,' Pavlik said, surveying me. 'But I'm afraid for me it's business this time.'

'Sheriff Pavlik responded to our call upon finding the unfortunate young lady's body yesterday,' Chitown said to Doty. 'And I must say, I've been very impressed. In Chicago, someone of your eminence would almost never be amongst the first responders.'

Before replying, Pavlik eyed Chitown evenly. 'We've had two other women—both also in real estate—found dead in my jurisdiction recently. Let's just say I take it a bit personally.'

Ward Chitown seemed a 'bit' stunned.

But Deirdre Doty said, 'That's so admirable—' gazing into my beau's blue-gray eyes—'I've heard about the realty agents who were killed. We had no idea that Brigid was the third, until Maggy here just told us.'

Pavlik cut a look toward me that didn't feel like a thank you.

Well, if I was a cat caught straying, I decided to drop the dead mouse in front of Pavlik by way of a peace offering. 'Deirdre met Brigid here Monday night.'

'So I've been told.' Our sheriff didn't look placated. You can't please everyone, even with a trophy-quality deceased rodent.

Given Doty's—to me, obvious—flirtation with the local law, Chitown seemed to be reappraising the relationship between Pavlik and me. 'Yes, I'm sure you've heard of the show we plan to film Saturday night. Deirdre, you did clear that with the sheriff's office?'

'Of course,' Doty said. 'I notified both Mr Pavlik's department as well as the Brookhills' municipal police. Sheriff, I believe I even spoke with your—' a hand laid on Pavlik's forearm—'community liaison?'

I eyed the leather being ever so subtly squeezed and idly wondered how heavy a meat cleaver I'd need to sever Doty's dallying hand at its wrist. 'According to the bartender, the two of them spoke at the bar from about 11:25 until just before midnight.'

But Pavlik ignored me. 'Mel told me about your request and everything is in order. I appreciate your going through the proper channels. A lot of event organizers don't seem to know what those are.'

Doty flushed with pleasure. 'Why, thank you, Sheriff.'

'Jake, please.'

Jake. I'd been bedding the man for more than a year, and I still called him 'Pavlik'. And Deirdre Doty'd better get her hand off his leather jacket, or I was going to find a suitable stand-in for that cleaver.

Chitown had gone from watching the interplay between Pavlik and me, to that between his own producer and the sheriff. 'Deirdre has been with me on a number of shoots. She's very good at what she does.'

The flush got deeper. 'It's simply a matter of knowing where to find information. In the case of Brookhills, I started with the historical society and Elaine Riordan was able to direct me to the proper authorities.' A quick scan of the room. 'In fact, I'm not sure where Elaine is. She said she'd meet us here tonight.'

'Did Elaine also "direct" you to Brigid at Kingston Realty?' I asked.

'In fact, she did,' Doty said. 'Elaine is a real estate broker, in addition to heading up the historical society, so she was able to track down which agent had the listing.'

Chitown's eyebrows tried to knit themselves a caterpillar. 'I thought you'd already done that. Online.'

'I did. The problem these days is that when you Google an address, you'll get hits from a lot of different real estate offices, but most won't be the listing agent. I originally contacted the Atherton Agency but because they weren't the listers, they would have had to contact what turned out to be Kingston Realty for access. Once she found out I wasn't looking to buy, she lost interest.'

'She? Do you mean Brigid?' I asked. I noticed Pavlik was hanging back, letting me ask the questions. He'd done it before, taking advantage of my friendships and, yes, knowledge of the community. He should be thanking me for my 'unrepentant, overly officious intermeddling'.

'No,' Deirdre replied. 'I was talking about Gabriella Atherton. She wasn't very nice when we spoke, I have to say. If I was Brigid, I'd think twice before going to work for her.'

'Oh.' A hand to the mouth, again, when Deirdre realized her faux-pas. 'I'm so sorry. For a second there, I forgot Brigid was, was…'

Pavlik patted her hand. 'It's very common for people to speak of the recently deceased in present tense. It doesn't mean you're being insensitive or callous.'

Yeah, yeah, Deirdre's a jewel beyond measure. Could we get back to the investigation?

'So,' I said, 'Brigid told you she intended to leave Kingston Realty in favor of Atherton Agency?'

'Not in so many words,' Doty said. 'But she did say she couldn't accompany me to meet Ward at the Ristorante because she was waiting for a prospective new employer.'

'So she sent you off on your own?' I asked.

'*With* the combination for the lockbox. I've booked a lot of shoots in vacant properties, but I've never had an agent give us free reign of the property without even going with us to look at the place.'

'You do have the property owner's permission to be there, I assume?' Pavlik asked.

'Owners, plural,' Deirdre answered. 'But of course. Which reminds me, Sheriff—'

'Jake,' I reminded her. Hey, we were all friends here, right?

'Jake,' Deirdre amended, ducking her head shyly.

'We'd like to get some footage of the room under the depot. Would that be permissible?'

'The scene has been released, so I don't see a problem with it.'

'Thank you.'

But on to more important matters. 'Deirdre, you just told us Brigid was waiting for a "prospective new employer",' I said. 'Did she say who?'

'No.' Doty paused for a beat. 'But I went to the restroom before I left the club and when I came out, Gabriella Atherton and Brigid were speaking in the foyer. The Atherton woman went back into the club proper, and Brigid trailed behind her. I put two and two together.'

'And you're certain it was Gabriella Atherton?' Honestly. The sheriff's department should be paying *me*.

'We'd only spoken by phone, but I recognized her from the billboards.'

Hard to hide when your face is ten-feet high overlooking the freeway.

DESPITE THAT, I never did manage to track down Gabriella Atherton, though I thought I caught a glimpse of Elaine Riordan finally arriving to meet Doty and Chitown.

'The bartender says Brigid and Gabriella talked together for only about fifteen minutes,' I told Pavlik as he waited in line with me for the valet to bring my car. I had his jacket draped across my shoulders against the cold night wind. 'Maybe the interview didn't go well.'

'So badly that Atherton crushed Ms Ferndale's skull somewhere and then moved the body to a hidey-hole under the depot's loading platform?'

I shrugged as a Lexus pulled up and the two women ahead of us stepped to the curb. 'Stranger things have happened.'

'True. And usually somewhere in proximity to you.' He checked his watch. 'This is taking forever. Why didn't you just self-park?'

'I was running late,' I said, 'for reasons you should well recall.'

I leaned into him and Pavlik slipped an arm around my waist, pulling me even closer. 'I certainly do,' he said in my ear. 'So why didn't you tell me you were coming here? We could have ridden together.'

I pulled back and looked at him. 'Really?'

A wince. 'Uh, no, actually. I was working.'

'Seems like I was doing all the work. You were sitting there letting Deirdre Doty have her way with your jacket.'

'You sound jealous,' Pavlik said as a BMW convertible pulled up and the valet hopped out. 'If only it was of me, instead of my—what do you call it?—buttery leather?'

'Folks?' the valet said, opening the passenger door of the Beamer.

I shook my head regretfully, as two people who'd been standing next to the building to stay warm brushed past us. 'You know I love both you *and* your leather.' I pulled the latter closer. 'Equally.'

Pavlik snickered. 'Thanks, Mom, but I do believe you love him—' he lifted the sleeve of the jacket— 'better than me.'

'What you can believe is that my feelings toward you are decidedly non-maternal,' I said, getting up on my tiptoes to give him a kiss on the cheek. 'So, will you really come to the after-show party?'

'I told Deirdre I would. Why? Are you invited, too?'

I punched his shoulder. 'Yes, I'm coming and I'll tell you, I'm going to dress appropriately this time.' In other words, as *in*appropriately as possible.

Pavlik looked at my outfit. 'You look fine.'

Fine. The way your mother says it. Not as in 'Damn, girl, you are looking fine!'

'Please,' I said. 'Did you see some of those dresses back there?'

'Sure, but you're ol...' He tried to cover his gaffe with a sudden, theatrical cough.

'I'm neither "old", nor dead,' I said, paraphrasing MaryAnne. 'And I am going to be drop-dead sexy Saturday night. As you'll see.'

'You are always drop-dead sexy,' he said, taking the opportunity to let his hand slip from my waist to my butt.

'Smoothly put, Sheriff,' I said, stepping away from him and sliding off the jacket. 'But methinks I have something to prove in two days' time.'

'Speaking of days, what do you have planned for tomorrow?' he said, taking the coat as my red Escape rolled into view.

In contrast to the arrival of the BMW, no one else stepped forward to claim it. In fact, I could have sworn the glitzy group took a collective half-step back.

Nonetheless, I loved my Ford. It sure beat the hell out of the battered mini-van I'd been driving last year.

'Maggy?' said Pavlik, a concerned look in his eyes.

'Uh, sorry. Zoning out for a second there. So, tomorrow? Friday I work the early shift and then I thought I'd go to the open house Sarah is having at MaryAnne Williams'. Want to come?' I asked, as Pavlik followed me around to the driver's side. 'I'm told there will be wine and cheese.'

'I think I'll pass, but you have a good time.' He tipped the valet and held the door for me. 'And I'm glad you'll be with Sarah. No real estate agent should be out in the world alone right now.'

'We'll use the buddy system.' I didn't mention Sarah's 'other' partners, Messrs Smith & Wesson. 'Did you have something else in mind for tomorrow night?'

'No,' he said, hand on my driver's side window sill. 'I have to work.'

I fastened my seatbelt. 'Then why did you ask?'

'Ask what?' Pavlik leaned down to give me a kiss goodbye.

'What I had planned for tomorrow. I thought you might want to do something...you know, get together?'

God, dating made me feel fourteen all over again. And I hadn't liked it very much that first time round.

'Nope.' The smile lit up his eyes. 'Just like to know your whereabouts, so I can alert the ground troops.'

My SUV's door closed firmly.

THIRTEEN

I NEEDED TO be at Uncommon Grounds by seven the next morning, and it was no mean feat just getting out of bed.

'I didn't fall asleep until nearly two,' I moaned to Frank as I scooched out from under the quilted comforter. 'Last time I had just four hours, Eric was still teething.'

The sheepdog didn't even bother to raise his head.

Just as well. If he roused himself, I would have had to take him out, and I wasn't sure I could muster the strength.

Still, I thought as I shuffled into the bathroom, I really had learned a lot and helped Pavlik, though I'm sure he wouldn't admit it.

My only disappointment was that, after losing sight of Gabriella Atherton, I never got a chance to talk with her. I fully intended to remedy that omission, though. Today was Friday and, according to MaryAnne, Gabriella's turn, again, to play in the Barbies' tennis foursome.

Making the real beauty of the situation Gabriella coming to me. I was sure Pavlik planned on having a conversation with Atherton himself today, but would he know where to find her at eight thirty (the tennis courts) or ten thirty (Uncommon Grounds)?

Well, Maggy does. And if the sheriff had just asked her, she would have told him.

Cranking up the shower and watching my third-person self climb in, I cringed as the water hit me. Gradually, though, it warmed and I started to feel human again. If only I could stay in the shower all day.

I finally stepped out and toweled myself down. My right palm was itching again and now showed little red bumps. A rash from the trumpet creeper, perhaps, though I hated to think Kate McNamara was right in her diagnosis. Or about anything, for that matter.

The newspaper woman hadn't been around much since the discovery of Brigid's body, but maybe her absence wasn't so surprising. *The Brookhills Observer* was only a weekly and normally hit the streets (OK, the convenience stores) Thursdays, meaning twenty-four hours ago.

Normally, also, that meant the deadline for submitting new stories would be Tuesday, but somehow I had a feeling Kate had made an exception, requiring her to spend yesterday in the *Observer*'s office working feverishly to dump articles like 'Preparing Your Garden for Winter' in favor of 'Local Woman Meets Violent Death'.

I applied Neosporin to ease the itching on my hand and edged into my closet.

The red of my palm did remind me of something.

I pawed through my collection of jeans. Some were boot-cut, some mom-cut, though I promised Eric I'd only wear those while working in the yard.

To which he'd said, '*Back*yard, Mom.'

What I didn't own were dress denims—certainly not the thousand-dollar-a-pair kind I'd seen at Sapphire or the 'skinny jeans' celebs wore on the glossy pages of magazines. I needed some simple dark-wash, straight-leg jeans I could pair with a chic little top for a night out.

But *not* tomorrow night.

Tomorrow night… I picked through the hangers in search of…ahh: red sheer stretch lace over a satin underlay just transparent enough to make people think they were seeing something they weren't. It was the perfect 'little red dress' and with the right slut shoes? Well, I thought the look could be dynamite.

Hell, I knew it was dynamite. Or had been a decade ago.

I moved the dress from the back of my closet to 'next-up' position and finished getting ready for work, buoyed by the fact I was going to look terrific at Sapphire.

I might be forty-five, but Diane Lane was a year older, Demi Moore, three years older still, and they both were gorgeous.

'Old', Sheriff Jake Pavlik? I'll give you old.

OUR MORNING COMMUTER rush was on as I arrived at Uncommon Grounds, so I didn't have a chance to talk with Tien about catering Chitown's party until after the second train had departed.

We were sitting at a deuce table, two lattes and the same of Tien's delicious pecan rolls in front of us.

'I'd be happy to do it, Maggy,' she said. 'I'll need help, though, so I hope my dad can get past his aversion to our Mafia past.'

Calling it 'our Mafia past' might not be the way to start the process.

'Do you know if anyone asked Luc for permission to shoot in the Ristorante?' I uncoiled a section of the sticky bun and popped a buttery piece into my mouth.

Mmmmm, heaven. I'd say just like mother used to make, but my mom was more into unsweetened granola and wheat germ. Everything tasted like dirt.

'Shoot?' Tien frowned. 'You mean like on Saturday?'

I nodded, given my mouth was full.

'Maggy, I'm honestly not even sure who owns the place. Are you?'

I swallowed. 'I guess I assumed your father did.'

'No. At least so far as I know. But as witnessed by the other night, I don't know much, even about my dad's side of our family.'

'If your grandmother just walked away from the property after your grandfather's death, I suppose it's possible the block reverted to Brookhills for back taxes. Or maybe the space was rented by your family and never owned. Either way, I get the impression your grandmother didn't want anything to do with it.'

'Ya think?' Tien, so exotically refined, nevertheless could lob sarcasm with the best of them.

'I think. I'll ask Sarah when I see her at MaryAnne Williams' open house this afternoon. If she was given the listing for the Ristorante, she'd have to know the identity of the seller. Or sellers.'

I expected another 'Ya think?', but Tien was chewing, so I received only a reciprocal nod of approval.

'But back to tomorrow,' I continued. 'Elaine Riordan will be calling later to tell you a guest count and talk some menu.'

'I hope she contacts me this morning. I'll want to

shop this afternoon, so I can begin cooking tomorrow—
oh, wait, will she be coming in today with her tennis
group?'

We both reflexively looked up at the three giant
clocks that dated from the old depot. The one set for
Brookhills said five minutes past ten. In other words,
nearly half-an-hour before Barbie saturation.

I relaxed. Plenty of time to figure out how I was
going to approach Gabriella Atherton. 'Elaine doesn't
play with the Friday group, though you could probably
reach her at the Historical Society rather than wait for
her to call you.'

'I think I will do that,' Tien said, getting up and
stacking our plates.

'Hey, I'm not done with that.' I salvaged my last
bite—the prized center with the glorious pocket of
gooey stuff in it.

Tien shook her head. 'I know what to get you for
Christmas, Maggy.'

'Sticky buns for life?'

'Sounds like the fitness infomercial from hell,' a
voice intoned.

My partner must have come in the platform door—
the one without chimes on it. I should bell the woman
the way a normal person would a bird-torturing cat.
'Thanks for scaring me. And what are you doing here?
This is your day off.'

'Day off to work my *other* job. No rest for the greedy.
What's the film crew doing out there?'

Oops. 'It's Chitown's people shooting footage of the
waiting room for the show tomorrow. You don't mind,
do you?'

'Would it stop you if I did?' My partner surveyed the plates in Tien's hands. 'All gone?'

'There's one in the bakery case.'

'I suppose I should leave that for the customers,' Sarah sniffed.

'Why start now? And besides—' I pointed at the glass-fronted cabinet—'Tien also made scones. They can have those.'

'Works for me.' Sarah pulled the last sticky bun from the case and brought it to the table.

'We were just talking about you,' I said as she settled into a chair at the next table, also a deuce.

'And who could blame you?' Like me, Sarah was un-coiling her sticky bun. Unlike me, though, she'd flipped the pastry upside down and was working counter-clock-wise.

A sin against sticky-bun nature. 'Who owns the Ris-torante?'

'Why do you ask?'

'Because I'm an intermeddler. Work with me on this.'

Instead of answering, Sarah addressed Tien. 'What else you got? Anything that will go with wine?'

'Wine?' Tien asked, looking at me.

I shrugged.

Sarah chewed the bun like a cow does cud. 'I'm doing an open house at the Williams this afternoon and MaryAnne wants me to serve wine and snacks.'

Tien said, 'Sounds like a fun way to sell a house.'

'The crowd will all be nosey neighbors,' Sarah re-plied. 'Open houses always are.'

'Then why schedule them?' I asked.

'The neighbors come, the neighbors go and then

you're done with them. Even they'd be embarrassed to waste your time by setting up a pretext appointment to see the place again.'

Made sense, I guessed. 'What time does this shindig start? I'm planning to come.'

Sarah did a double-take. 'Why?'

'To prevent someone from shooting you. Is that OK?'

'I suppose. But what if they shoot both of us?'

'I'll take my chances. Now what time?'

'Four to six.'

Tien said, 'So you'll need finger food, Sarah?'

'Gosh, I don't know. MaryAnne is going to be at some design show this afternoon and won't arrive until five, but she told me there'd be wine in the kitchen. I figured to maybe just pick up a container of that spray cheese at Pick 'n Save. And, of course, celery sticks.'

Tien and I looked at each other and then at Sarah.

'What?' she asked, looking somewhere between innocent and peeved.

'Gosh,' I parroted, 'you're splurging with spray cheese *and* celery sticks, why not break the bank and get a sleeve of Ritz crackers, too.'

Those being, admittedly, my cracker of choice with spray cheese.

'It's fine,' Tien said. 'Sarah, I have some things in the cooler that I think will work well with wine. I'll put together a couple of appetizing trays.'

'Shame on you, holding spray cheese over her head like that,' I said to my partner after Tien disappeared into the kitchen. 'You *knew* she wouldn't let you embarrass yourself and besmirch Uncommon Grounds' reputation, by extension. No matter *how* much she has to do for tomorrow.'

'Why? What's tomorrow?'

Dang. A couple more things I'd forgotten to mention to my business partner. I filled Sarah in on the catering job, as well as our invitation to Ward Chitown's live show and celebration afterwards.

'Sure, I'll come. What are they celebrating?' Sarah was still eating and didn't mind talking with her mouth full. In fact, she seemed to prefer, even revel, in it.

'The end of the show? The discovery of the loot? Either way, I'm in.' And wearing my red dress.

'So, have you seen Pavlik?'

'Yup. He'll be at the party, too.'

'And?'

Sarah took an interest in my love life—mostly because she thought I mismanaged it.

I said, '*And* he stopped over last night after work and I also ran into him at Sapphire later on.'

'And?'

'And, well—' I could feel myself color up—'I was in the shower when he—'

'Not that, you idiot,' Sarah exploded. 'What did he tell you? And I'm not talking about how you looked in Scrubbing Bubbles.'

Seemed uncalled for. 'I assume you mean about Brigid?'

Sarah just glared at me.

'He said that she was killed by a blow to the head somewhere else and then moved to the waiting room.'

I'd expected Sarah to be relieved but, if anything, she appeared more concerned. 'Moved *here*?'

'Not a bad spot, when you think about it. If that vent in the bathroom hadn't conducted the smell, we might never have known there was a waiting area down there, much less that Brigid was moldering inside it.'

'True.' Sarah seemed to be chewing more on her thoughts than on her bun. Which was saying something.

'OK.' I finally asked. 'What?'

'"What" is the wrong question, Maggy.' She looked up. 'Someone killed my employee and then moved her corpse to this "secret" room in a building I own. The obvious question is, why?'

FOURTEEN

THE OBVIOUS ANSWER? To frame Sarah for the killing of an employee who ratted out her employer to the state board governing Sarah's license to make a living. But even that begged the same question.

Why?

'No idea,' Sarah said, back to chewing before I posed a second observation.

'Since it's possible that Brigid was attacked while on the job, Pavlik thinks the three killings could be related.'

'Well, duh.'

My day for sarcasm from everybody. How's one supposed to brainstorm in the face of such judgmental put-downs?

Sarah took a break from her sticky bun. 'So, does your sheriff like me for all three murders?'

Sometimes I wasn't sure Pavlik liked Sarah at all, but I went with her cop jargon. 'Not really. In fact, he was glad I was going to be with you at the open house. He said no realty agent should be in a property alone until we collar this killer.'

'"Until *we* collar the killer"?' Sarah repeated. 'I just bet he said that. Besides, anything Pavlik tells you is probably to throw me off. Create a false sense of security in his primary suspect.'

She pushed her plate away, which might have been

interpreted as loss of appetite if the thing hadn't been virtually vacuumed clean. 'Before long, he'll have you wearing a wire.'

'So he can listen while you kill me?'

'Why would I do that? You're not in real estate.'

'Sarah, I hope the question by now should be, why would you kill anyone?'

The bells on the street-side door jingled before she could answer. Enter Gabriella Atherton, Jane Smith, and the blonde who had been with the group on Wednesday, when Brigid's body had been discovered. Redhead, brunette and blonde—all wearing tennis whites. Missing was MaryAnne Williams.

'I'm going,' Sarah said, following me as I circled behind the counter to take the Barbies' order. 'Bring the food when you come.'

'Me?' In one fell swoop, Sarah had successfully suckered Tien into making the snacks for the open house and me, apparently, into delivering them.

'Sure,' Sarah said. 'Why should I wait and then have to take them to MaryAnne's or home until this afternoon when you can just bring them from here?'

Made sense. Damn it. 'What time?'

'The house opens at the stroke for four p.m. I'll be arriving at three thirty, so you should be there by three forty-five, latest.'

I should and, of course, I would. This was Sarah, after all. Resistance was futile and, in this case, unnecessary. 'Amy is relieving me at three, so that'll work out fine.'

Gabriella Atherton was chomping at her bit on the other side of our service window. I wasn't sure if it was because she resented Kingston Realty having the listing for MaryAnne's house or because the competing broker just badly needed a jolt of caffeine.

As my partner went through the kitchen and presumably out the back, I addressed our customers. 'Morning, ladies. How was your tennis today?'

'Awful!' This from Jane Smith. 'First of all, Fox Ears requires white tennis attire, which eliminates most of my favorite outfits. Then MaryAnne and I lost at love and love.'

'Georgia and I played that team a couple of weeks ago,' Atherton said. 'They kept lobbing us.'

'And both of them stay back,' the blonde contributed. 'What fun is that?'

'MaryAnne didn't continue on with you for coffee?' I began frothing skim milk in preparation for their drink orders.

'No, she had to make sure everything is ready for the open house because she also has a design show today.' Smith was holding a menu, which she'd been studying as she spoke. 'Oh, I don't know why I even look anymore. I'll have my usual, Maggy.'

Ahh, yes. The latte that's not a latte. How very Zen of her.

I made it first, then a flavored coffee for the blonde, saving Gabriella's drink for last. 'Iced latte?'

'Please. Light on the ice.'

'Of course.' I tamped the espresso into the portafilter and then lowered my voice. 'I assume you've heard that it was Brigid Ferndale whose body was found.'

'I did.' Instead of a chilly tone, Atherton leaned in

conspiratorially. 'I have to say I was a little surprised to see Sarah here today.'

Did she mean 'instead of jail'? I would've asked, but I wanted information and knew from experience that you can catch more Barbies with honey or, more likely, Splenda, given their obsession with calorie-counting. 'She's very concerned, as I'm sure you are.'

'Me?'

'About the safety of your agents,' I said, setting down the portafilter, rather than twisting it on the espresso machine. 'You know: the three women who've been killed?'

'Of course, I know.' Atherton stared hard at our filter. 'Luckily, none have been from my firm. I've been telling them to be very careful. Always work in pairs.'

I glanced back over my shoulder, as if I were making sure my partner couldn't overhear. 'What a double shame, then, that Brigid hadn't made the move to Atherton yet.'

Atherton's eyes could have ignited a brush fire. 'What do you mean?'

'I mean, if you and she had come to an agreement on Monday night, Brigid might be alive today.'

'Really.' Neutral. Neither agreement or disagreement. 'Aren't you going to make my drink?'

'Oh, sorry.' I feigned surprise and twisted the filter on the machine.

'Anyway,' I continued, 'Brigid told me in confidence—' another glance around for an invisible Sarah— 'that she was interested in joining your firm.'

'She did?' Now one eyebrow went up. 'Why would Brigid tell you that?'

'Please.' I pushed the button for the espresso and pulled the cold, nonfat milk from the refrigerator. 'If anyone knows how difficult Sarah can be, it's me.'

Forgive me, Sarah. Though, it was undeniably true—just not a sentiment I'd share with Gabriella or anyone else for that matter. Sarah was like a hangnail. Annoying, yes; aggravating, often. But you never questioned the fact you had a hand.

But I wax philosophical and thus digress.

Atherton shrugged. 'Brigid and I did speak for a few minutes at Sapphire on Monday, but I really can't afford to bring anyone on who doesn't already have solid connections in the community.'

The definition of a potential rainmaker, as Mary-Anne Williams had put it.

'Brigid must have known at least Kingston Realty's clients.' Dumping the espresso in a glass, I added milk. 'From what I could tell, she was practically running the place.'

'Perhaps. However, as I tried to explain to Brigid, that doesn't mean the clients would—or even legally *could*—follow her to Atherton.'

'I suppose she didn't believe you. I liked her, but Brigid came across a little too…'

'Full of herself?' Atherton said, pushing me a Splenda to supplement her drink. 'I'd have to agree. Brigid practically bragged that she could take down Kingston Realty. Single-handedly.' A tight smile. 'Ballsy. It made me want to give her a chance. Almost.'

As Atherton opened her handbag to pay me, stirring chords from Richard Wagner's 'Ride of the Valkyries'— the signature theme played during the sky cavalry's helicopter attack on a Vietnamese village in the movie *Apocalypse Now*—rang out from inside the designer leather.

Atherton dug like a badger. Instead of her wallet, she pulled out a smart phone. 'Gabriella Atherton.'

She listened. 'I'm sorry, but you're breaking up a bit. I'm at…yes…you've changed your…? But what about…?' A glance at me. 'Of course, dear. I'll run right over.'

'Need a to-go cup?' I asked, wondering if Gabriella still got the same rush, as MaryAnne put it, from assignations with Robert as she had when they were cheating on his wife.

'Yes, please.' She stuck the phone back in her bag and this time did pull out her wallet.

'Would you like me to remove the ice?' Better to do it as I was pouring into the new cup, rather than trying to fish the cubes out after.

'No, no. It's fine.' She slapped a five down on the counter, grabbing for the drink. 'I need to run.'

'Cover?' I said, holding a clear plastic one in my hand. 'So it doesn't slop all over your Mercedes?'

'Please.'

I held the cover where it was. 'Did Brigid tell you where she was going after you spoke?'

'Going?' Impatience was palpable in her voice.

'When Brigid left Sapphire Monday night.' I tamped the lid at strategic points on the cup's rim, but kept my fingers atop it.

Atherton shook her head, impatience now evidently growing inside her, as well. 'Brigid wanted fifteen minutes of my time and I gave it to her. Then I went to join some friends and, so far as I know, our little schemer returned to the bar.'

Gabriella Atherton pulled the drink away from me and, with a machine-gun explanation whispered to her friends, left.

IT WAS PAST noon now, yet I was still thinking about what Gabriella Atherton had said.

She'd given Brigid fifteen minutes of her time. What Brigid had done after that—with the remainder of the time the young woman had on earth, as it turned out—was anybody's guess.

Except the killer's.

According to Benjy the bartender, Brigid had spoken with Deirdre Doty until about midnight. Then, this time according to Gabriella Atherton, the two women had spoken for fifteen minutes. After that, Atherton said that Brigid returned to the bar where—back to Benjy—she'd closed out at twenty minutes after midnight and presumably left, never to be seen again.

Could Brigid have been abducted from the parking lot? If so, her car should have still been there.

Unless, of course, she'd been the victim of a car-jacking.

I picked up my cell and pushed '1' on its speed-dial. Nothing happened. Then I pushed 'P' and held it down. New smartphone, not-so-smart new owner. 'Pav... I mean, Jake, this is Maggy.'

'Good try, Maggy, but I've gotten used to Pavlik. What's up?'

His voice, warm though it was, sounded hurried, so I cut to the chase. 'Has Brigid's car been found?'

A pause. 'Why do you ask?'

Where had I heard that before? 'Because I was talk-ing to Gabriella Atherton and—'

'What a surprise.' You could tell from the tone of his voice that it wasn't.

'She stopped in for coffee,' I explained. 'Said how sad it was about Brigid. And how much she'd wanted to work for Gabriella.'

'Ms Atherton volunteered that?'

'Well, I guess I might have said it first,' I admitted, 'but Gabriella confirmed it.'

'As she did when I spoke with her.'

So Pavlik *had* tracked her down, presumably before tennis. 'Well, then you also know that Gabriella stayed at Sapphire with friends after Brigid left. It occurred to me that Brigid must have driven there, but I don't re-member hearing anything about her car.'

A hesitation. Then: 'The car was found in a slot near Uncommon Grounds, Maggy. We towed it to the crime lab's garage yesterday to check the vehicle for trace evidence.'

The white Toyota MaryAnne and I had seen go by on the flatbed truck. 'What did you find?. If you can tell me, of course.'

'We didn't find much, but there's no way that Brigid Ferndale was killed in her car.'

I ARRIVED AT MaryAnne Williams' house just a minute shy of four. When Amy had arrived to take over the shop, she'd asked for an update. Since I'd neglected to call our intrepid barista before she walked into a full-blown murder investigation the day before, I figured I owed her more than a cursory: Brigid bludgeoned, body moved, murderer at large.

Besides, there was that whole people-person issue.

It was nearly three thirty when Amy had helped me carry two platters of appetizers out to the Escape. I'd stopped home and let Frank out—food still safely sealed in the Escape—and then proceeded to the open house.

Or, open mansion.

MaryAnne Williams' place was on Wildwood Drive, the same street where my ex-husband, Ted, had lived with his second wife. Wildwood was off Poplar Creek Road, but, instead of turning east, toward Ted's, I turned west on Wildwood toward Poplar Creek, the stream itself.

I'd been to MaryAnne's home once for a Historical Society fund-raiser and, unlike many of the McMansions in this southernmost—and toniest—part of Brookhills, it wasn't sandwiched in amongst other monstrosities. Instead, the house stood proudly at the center of a two-acre plot that bordered on the creek.

I parked my car behind Sarah's in the driveway, noticing that there was a third car, a Mercedes, in front of that. It looked like Gabriella Atherton's but then so did every other big, black Mercedes. Besides, what would Atherton be doing here?

Climbing out of my Escape, I opened the rear liftgate and considered trying to carry both platters. Nah. I was already late, but arriving with road-kill appetizers trailing behind me? Sarah would take that pistol... sorry, *revolver*, to my skull.

I carefully slid one tray out, leaving the lift gate up. My plan was to ring the doorbell, hand over the one platter to Sarah, and then run back to get the other, along with my handbag.

Only problem? No answer from inside.

Then again, maybe no bell had actually rung. Not wanting to take a chance on losing the platter, I'd punched the button with an elbow.

Now I set the tray down on a small, wrought-iron table to one side of the door and pressed the button again. This time, an audible, if muffled, ding-dong.

But still, no Sarah.

Opening the aluminum storm, I saw the lockbox dangling from the handset of the heavy wooden door. Knocking, I stepped back to survey the house.

Pink brick and really very charming, despite its size. I knew the inside to be the same. Six thousand square feet, but every room felt just right. Not overpowering, almost…cozy.

Around the back was a swimming pool surrounded by a tiled patio. From the fringe of the pool apron, a wide expanse of lawn sloped down to the creek. The day of the fund-raiser in June, white tables with umbrellas had spotted both the pool deck and the lawn while a string quartet played beneath the tallest weeping willow tree I had ever seen.

I peeked around a corner of the house, but all I could see was MaryAnne's high—not to mention legally-required—fence of wrought iron surrounding her pool.

Still no response at the door, and I was growing worried about Sarah. I left Tien's platter of cheese cubes, vegetable tarts and miniature sandwiches to fend for themselves and followed the flagstoned path that led to the rear.

Because I'd arrived late, Sarah had likely been there a good thirty minutes before. The Mercedes, given that Sarah had boxed it in, must already have been on-site when she came. Had my business partner walked in on something? Or, had someone arrived earlier, hidden in the house and taken her by surprise?

Though if you were intending to be an assailant, parking your Mercedes where it could be road-blocked in the driveway didn't seem part of a smart getaway plan.

The path brought me to a gate I hadn't remembered seeing, though admittedly I'd come through the house that day, the better for Elaine Riordan and her minions to force you past the silent auction tables in the living room.

I pushed on the gate and was surprised when it swung easily open. Maybe the pool cleaners or lawn people had left it that way but, if so, MaryAnne needed to talk with them. Ted and I had maintained a large 'umbrella' insurance policy just because of our pool, but no amount of liability coverage would ever have made up for an accident resulting from carelessness.

I closed the gate tight behind me, making sure the lock engaged. I was fighting a building sense of panic. Three real estate agents had been killed and I couldn't reach Sarah.

Should I call Pavlik?

Except…my smartphone was in my purse, which was next to the second platter in the back of the Escape.

I stopped, suddenly and desperately wanting to regain the safety of the front driveway where I could access my cell and be sure I had a getaway route of my own, while still blocking in the other two cars until help arrived.

But could the Mercedes belong to MaryAnne? Maybe she'd driven a different vehicle or gotten a ride to her other event. Or maybe she'd skipped it altogether.

So what if I telephoned Pavlik and he sent the troops, as he had called them? Deputies would find me cowering in the Escape, doors locked and windows up. Inside, of course, Sarah and MaryAnne would be opening the wine and arranging cocktail napkins, music turned up so high that they couldn't hear...

A high-pitched scream pierced the stillness.

The cry had come from the back of the house. Forgetting about my cellphone and the cars and the trays of appetizers, I sprinted down the walkway to a break in the row of arbor vitae that surrounded the patio proper. As I did, I registered that the shriek I'd heard had not belonged to Sarah.

Should I be glad? I didn't know, since at least the screamer, presumably, was still alive.

As was Sarah. As I broke through the hedge, I saw my business partner standing at the edge of the pool with another woman... Jane Smith?

The brunette, body language projecting horror, was backing away from Sarah. 'What... What did you...?'

For her part, Sarah was doing...well, pretty much nothing.

I pulled even with her, me gasping for air. 'What's wrong?'

Sarah pointed.

I turned to see a redhaired woman in tennis whites, floating face down in the pool.

FIFTEEN

No more information seemed forthcoming from Sarah, so I turned to Jane Smith. 'What happened?'

'I don't know,' said Smith. 'I came back here and saw her—' she pointed at Sarah—'and then…her.'

'So no one has…' I broke off, not wanting to waste the time. Instead, I kicked off my shoes and jumped into the pool, ignoring the shock of the frigid water.

It only took two strokes to reach the woman. I'd taken life-saving when Ted and I had bought the house with the swimming pool, but that was a very long time ago. Still, I knew enough to grasp the victim and roll same onto her back.

If the red hair had been a strong clue, the face proved a giveaway.

Gabriella Atherton. There went my burgeoning theory that she'd been the one to kill Brigid Ferndale and try to pin it on Sarah.

Slipping an arm under Gabriella's chin to tow her, I managed, 'Call 9-1-1,' as I side-stroked to the pool's long side.

No one moved.

'Call…9-1-1!' I sputtered on pool water.

This time, Sarah stirred. 'I—'

'Sarah!' I said, reaching the stairs of the pool. 'Call Pavlik, *now*!'

She nodded once and dug into the bulging pockets of her 'uniform' jacket.

Meanwhile, I signaled Jane Smith. 'Help me get out.'

To the woman's credit, she came forward, but shrunk back as she leaned down to grasp Atherton's shoulders. 'What's that?'

She was pointing at the woman whose face I still held above water, despite the fact I feared it was too late.

An irregular pattern of stippling and, at its center, a dark hole in Gabriella Atherton's temple.

The EMTs arrived first and took over. Though I'd started CPR—more pool-owner training—I hadn't detected any response from the victim.

One of the emergency workers had seen I was wet and gave me a blanket to wrap around myself against the cold. As Jane Smith and I stood back to watch the med-techs work, I asked Sarah the same question I'd put just fifteen minutes earlier. 'What happened?'

'I don't know. I went through the house to make sure everything was in order and put out the sell sheets on every flat surface. Then I came back to the kitchen and opened MaryAnne's wine.

'When you still weren't here, I checked out back, because I'd asked MaryAnne not to close the pool for the winter so the house would show better. I wanted to make sure the water looked clean and nothing disgusting was...'

Floating, I finished for her mentally.

I'd pulled countless mice, voles, squirrels and even the occasional snake or crawfish out of Ted's and my pool. This, glancing toward the EMTs, was far, far worse.

'And Gabriella was already in the pool?'

Sarah nodded. 'At first I didn't understand what I was seeing, then she—' pointing to Smith—'came up behind me, screaming. And who are you, anyway?'

'Sarah, Jane's one of our customers at Uncommon Grounds.' Though, given I'd served the woman for a year without knowing her name, I didn't have the right to register proprietary indignation at my business partner. 'Jane Smith.'

I turned to Smith. 'So Gabriella and you were both already here when Sarah arrived?'

The brunette blinked. 'No. Why would you think that?'

'Because there's only one car and it's parked in front of Sarah's. I assumed you made plans this morning at tennis to come here together.' I was pretty proud of my clear reasoning, given I was shivering from a combination of the cold and the dissipating adrenaline rush.

'The last time I saw Gabriella was in your shop, when she left to meet a client.' Smith's eyes kept flicking sideways toward her friend surrounded by EMTs. 'Besides, I walked over.'

I let the supposed 'client' pass. 'Walked? Where do you live?'

Smith blushed. 'Just on the other side of Poplar Creek Road.'

'So you're a neighbor.' Sarah was searching her pockets, presumably for cigarettes. 'What did I tell you, Maggy?'

Nosy neighbors poking around open houses were the

least of our worries right now. Sarah's main business competitor was dead, evidently of unnatural causes. In that, Gabriella Atherton joined three other women in the field, which included one who had reported her boss—my coffee shop partner—to the real estate licensing board.

I didn't think Sarah was ridding the world of agents.

But someone sure was.

THE SHERIFF'S DEPARTMENT followed on the heels of the EMTs. They taped off the area and moved us back, then interviewed each of us separately. I was first, and now Sarah Kingston and Jane Smith were talking to their respective deputies.

Pavlik arrived just as the crime-scene investigators started their work.

He came over to me. 'Are you all right?'

'Fine,' I lied. In truth, I was freezing, but I was damned if I was going to leave as the deputies had told me I was free to do.

'I'm just sorry I was late, so Sarah had to find—' I pointed to the gurney that held Gabriella Atherton's body bag—'this alone.'

'Honestly?' Pavlik said. 'It would be good for Sarah if there were another witness, but I'm glad you were late. The less you're involved, the better.' He tugged the blanket tighter around me.

'You can't think Sarah did this.'

My partner's gun had been confiscated—or better, voluntarily surrendered.

'Ms Atherton and the other two shooting victims had wounds consistent with a much smaller caliber bullet than that .357 Smithy pocket cannon your friend was packing.'

I brightened. 'So, she couldn't have done it.'

'Not with that revolver. For now, though, that's all I can say.'

For now, it was enough.

'My Lord!' a woman's voice said from inside the house. 'What in the world is going on?'

MaryAnne Williams swept into her backyard, a sheriff's deputy guiding more than guarding her.

Pavlik left me to introduce himself.

MaryAnne extended her hand. 'Of course I remember you, Sheriff. You were Maggy's escort for our little fund-raiser here. And a very dashing one, as I recall?'

But the Southern courtesy of our former Atlanta belle proved to be short-lived. 'I don't understand, Sheriff. The deputy who met me at the door said there has been a shooting?'

Before Pavlik could answer, MaryAnne registered my appearance. 'Maggy, whatever are you doing here? And looking like a drowned rat to boot?'

'Umm…well…' I pointed to Pavlik. 'You'd better ask him.'

But MaryAnne had seen Sarah, interview apparently over. Jane Smith seemed to be finishing up with her deputies, as well, all the while throwing worried looks toward MaryAnne.

Who, in turn, was crushing my surprised partner in an embrace. 'Sarah, honey, thank God. I was afraid this crazed killer had gotten you and it was somehow all my fault.'

Sarah didn't crush easily. And she responded to hugs

even less. 'I'm fine. And, if I had been shot, why would that be your fault?'

Not a bad question.

'Because I insisted you handle my open house personally?'

'I didn't have much choice.' Sarah spread her hands out wide. 'These days I'm a one-woman operation.' She glanced over at me. 'At least the realty side of my life.'

I was genuinely touched by Sarah's evident relief at having me around for backup. In oh-so-many ways.

MaryAnne began looking around. 'But if you're unhurt, then who...?'

'Gabriella Atherton,' Pavlik said. 'She was found dead in your pool.'

'Gabriella?' MaryAnne tilted her head. 'What in the world would she be doing here?'

Smith, who'd been heading toward us, made a U-turn and quickstepped out the gate.

'You mean Jane Smith?' I asked.

'Jane? No.' Apparently MaryAnne hadn't seen her neighbor. 'I meant Gabriella.'

'We were hoping you'd know why Ms Atherton might have come by,' Pavlik said. 'I understand you played tennis together. Might she have just...dropped in?'

'I very much doubt that. We didn't really see much of each other outside of tennis? And, besides, why would she be in my backyard?'

'Looking at the property?' Pavlik ventured. 'Maybe she was interested in taking over the listing.'

'Interested? Well, I guess that's certainly possible,' MaryAnne said. 'But I made it clear to her—and to

just about *every*body—that my listing was staying with
Kingston Realty, so long as Sarah owned it.'

'So long as she owned it?' I repeated, turning to
Sarah. 'Have you been thinking of selling?'

'Not until—' an expansive wave that included both
MaryAnne's pool and Gabriella's gurney—'now.'

MaryAnne shrugged. 'Perhaps I misunderstood. Gabriella said something about the difficulty of remaining
licensed in the realty area when you had irons in other
fires? I assumed that she meant Sarah was concentrat-
ing on the coffeehouse.'

My partner's eyes narrowed. I felt Sarah and I were
weathervanes pointing in the same direction: Brigid
Ferndale and Gabriella Atherton had been in cahoots.
Maybe getting Sarah's real estate license revoked was
the dowry Brigid was bringing to the imminent business marriage. With Sarah off the board as a competitor, all her clients would be up for grabs.

For the first time, I wondered whether Sarah's employee, Theodore, really had sexually harassed Brigid,
or if that was just another part of her master plan.

Nah. Theo was a pig.

'Did Gabby Girl mention Brigid by name?' Sarah
was demanding.

'Gabby Girl? Oh, you mean Gabriella.' MaryAnne's
expression, puzzled at the nickname, now slid toward a
grin. 'I'd pay money to see her face if...'

MaryAnne trailed off self-consciously, probably
approaching the same painful, brain-cramp territory
that Deirdre Doty had last night when talking to Pavlik about Brigid Ferndale.

Moving the recently deceased from our present tense and into the past.

I cleared my throat. 'I think what Sarah was asking was whether Gabriella ever mentioned Brigid to you.'

'No, but she still worked for you, Sarah, so—'

Pavlik jumped in. 'Ms Williams, did Ms Atherton's realty have a key to your house?'

'No, of course not. Kingston has the only key.'

Now Pavlik to Sarah. 'And you used that to gain entrance today?'

'I did, though I didn't bring the key with me. We keep it in a lockbox on the front door.' Sarah seemed to sense something from the sheriff. 'And that's standard practice throughout the industry.'

Pavlik nodded. 'Anyone else have the combination, then?'

'No, I—'

'Brigid would have,' I interrupted. 'And maybe she gave it to Gabriella.'

'But why ever would Brigid do that?' MaryAnne asked.

Her guess was as good as mine and, seemingly, neither of us had even that. 'I don't know, MaryAnne, though maybe it's neither here nor there. Gabriella wouldn't have needed the key just to access the backyard.'

MaryAnne looked puzzled and turned. 'But she had to come through the house, Maggy.' A turn back. 'I always keep my gates locked, and that fence is six-feet high. I doubt Gabriella scaled it.'

'Sorry, but that gate—' I gestured—'was unlocked.

It's how I got in. I assumed the pool cleaners or some-body left it open.'

'Impossible.' MaryAnne was shaking her head em-phatically. 'Both my yard and pool services came by this morning to do a spruce-up toward the open house. I checked that gate when I stopped home after tennis, as I always do after they've been here. Their men do a wonderful job on the grounds, but they're not as secu-rity conscious as one might hope.'

Pavlik addressed me. 'Yet you're certain the gate was unlocked?'

'Positive. It wasn't even closed completely. Mary-Anne, opposite question: someone could have gotten *out* of the yard, even if the gate *was* locked, right?'

'Yes, yes—the lock is to keep people out, honey, not in. And my attorney told me I couldn't prevent egress from the property, in case of fire or whatever. Are you thinking the killer escaped that way?'

'If the person was in a hurry,' I said, 'he or she might not have pulled the gate closed behind them, meaning the lock wouldn't have engaged. It explains my being able to go through the gate, even though you'd secured it earlier.'

It also indicated that someone was on the scene be-fore Sarah. A good thing, since my partner could be for-given for having murderous thoughts about both Brigid and Gabriella, who now appeared to have been conspir-ing against her.

Except Sarah hadn't known about their scheme. Or, at least, I assumed she hadn't.

I rubbed my forehead with the heel of both hands.

Pavlik noticed the gesture. 'Maggy, you and Sarah

are free to go. I would like to talk to you for a moment, though,' he said, nodding toward MaryAnne.

I put my hand on the older woman's shoulder. 'Are you going to be all right here alone tonight? I have a guest room.'

Though she'd have to share it with a sheepdog.

'Thank you, Maggy, but I'll be fine. And if I get the heebie-jeebies, I'll call my sister or maybe Elaine. I have to say though—' her eyes slid toward the gurney being lifted for transport—'I think I'll leave the crime-solving to you, from now on.'

She gave off a shiver.

IF MARYANNE FOLLOWED either option, she must have reached her sister, because I arrived at Uncommon Grounds the next morning to find Elaine Riordan with Tien in our storeroom.

It was Saturday, a relatively slow day for a business like ours that catered to the commuter crowd. We'd even experimented with abandoning weekends altogether, but had finally compromised on short hours—7 a.m. to 12 noon—on Saturday, closed on Sunday.

'What do you think, Maggy?' Tien asked. 'Should we serve the cold beverages today in Styrofoam or clear plastic cups?'

'Styrofoam,' I said, without missing a beat. 'Our logo will show up better against the white background.'

'That's genius,' Riordan said, looking up from the yellow-lined pad of paper on which she was jotting notes. 'Oh, and both Deirdre and Ward want you each to get as much product-placement value as possible, given that we're just paying out-of-pockets.'

'I'll be finished here at noon,' I said. 'What can I do to help?'

'We're setting up the buffet in the Ristorante's dining room,' Tien said. 'I haven't had a chance to get over there, but Elaine has described it and also says the kitchen is in fairly good shape.'

Our anorexic blonde was nodding. 'I wouldn't want to cook a gourmet meal there, certainly. But there is reliable running water and working appliances as well.

'We'll need to feed the film crew around four?' Riordan continued. 'That way they can be back to work by five, so we can begin to take care of our guests.'

'How many locals have you invited?' I asked.

'Not all that many—perhaps ten or fifteen. The show is live, so we'll all need to trail after the hand-held cameras through the Ristorante, the slaughterhouse and God knows where else. Still, Ward wants to thank those who've helped us the most—you and your partner, the sheriff and his public information people, a few county and town officials. Oh, and Kate McNamara and the rest of the print reporters, of course.'

'No television?' I asked, a little disappointed. A logo on the cups wouldn't do any good if no one was there to film them.

'Heavens no. WTVR, the local affiliate airing the show, wouldn't hear of it. They want exclusive first dibs on whatever Ward might find.'

The excitement of being involved with the production seemed to agree with Riordan. There was a flush of excitement on her hollow cheeks and even her reedy voice was stronger.

'Live at seven, right?' I needed to set my DVR. I was

also trying to figure out how I could help with food and wander through a slaughterhouse, all the while wearing my red slut dress.

Maybe there'd be time to go home and change after the show, but before the party.

'Seven to eight, and then Sapphire is opening early for us right after that. Although if all goes well, we may be delayed by the rest of the media clamoring for interviews to air on their ten o'clock news shows.'

Elaine probably had a triumphant Ward Chitown in mind, brandishing a big satchel of money. I was thinking more Maggy Thorsen in her stunning red dress, holding up an Uncommon Grounds cup, logo toward lens.

Maybe I'd stick the dress and shoes in a bag and change en route. Regardless, at the stroke of noon I planned to rush home, let Frank out and shower the caffeine from my hair and pores.

'So if I arrive around one thirty, is that OK?' I asked.

'Sure,' Tien said. 'Jacque is going to help, too. He's made some wonderful stuffed clams and mini crab-cakes we're going to serve along with a clam chowder.'

If I thought Elaine had been glowing, she was a dim bulb compared to Tien.

'Yum,' I said. 'What about your dad?'

A subtle shake of the head, with her eyes slewing toward Riordan. 'He's busy, so that's why Jacque is helping.'

Luc Romano didn't want to be around what I'm sure he believed was a glorification of an event that had negatively marked his family and changed their lives forever. I understood and I knew Tien did, too.

'Elaine and I are going to start taking things over to the Ristorante now,' Tien continued.

'Want to use the Escape?' I asked, pulling the keys out of my pocket and dangling them.

'That would be wonderful,' she said, gratefully taking them. 'My VW bug won't hold much of anything. C'mon, Elaine.'

But the other woman stayed back as Tien left our storeroom. 'I'll be right there.'

When Tien was out of earshot, Elaine said, 'Mary-Anne called last night and told me what happened at her house.'

'Was she shook up?' I asked.

Riordan thought about it. 'Not so much upset as maybe…intrigued? Like all of us, she'd heard about the attacks on agents, though this one struck far too close to home.'

Literally and figuratively.

'MaryAnne made me promise not to show any houses by myself.' Riordan gave a little shiver and I half-expected her to pull out her afghan. 'I guess it's a good thing I'm a terrible sales associate.'

'I'm sure that's not true.' A fib.

'Oh, but it is.' Riordan was going through her handbag, but no afghan—or even a Chihuahua—was in evidence. 'I thought I'd be helping people find their dream homes, but…well, it's a lot more cutthroat than that.'

She didn't have to tell me. 'Did you stay with Mary-Anne last night?'

'No.' Riordan managed to tug tissues from her bag. And not a single one, mind you, nor even just a purse-size packet. A whole, frickin' box. 'MaryAnne was worried about me, not the other way around. Besides, I think I bother her when I stay. I tend to be a bit of a hypochondriac.'

Riordan plucked a tissue and blew her nose. Ten seconds, three octaves.

'Well, anyway,' I said, now trying to distance myself from contagion, 'it seems like you've been very helpful to Ward Chitown and his producer.'

'I'm a gofer,' Riordan said, wedging the box back into her bag, splitting one of the cardboard's corner seams, 'but it seems I'm good at it. I'm thinking if I show a little initiative, I could train to become a producer like Deirdre.'

'Sounds like it's an interesting job.' I was leading the way from the storeroom back into the kitchen. 'I'm sure you—'

I was interrupted by the 'brrring' of an old-fashioned telephone. Riordan dove back into her bag, temporarily stymied by the tissue box and God-knew-what-else until she found her cell, sneezed again, and said, 'Hello?'

Wanting to give her privacy—not to mention getting away from a germ-spewing looney—I signaled Elaine I was going out front.

She nodded to me. 'Yes, I did,' she said into the phone. 'But where did you say…?'

Her words trailed away as I thought of the call Gabriella Atherton had gotten in my presence, late yesterday morning. What was it she said?

I thought she'd addressed the person on the other end of the line by 'dear' and said something about 'running right over'?

Had Atherton gone to meet Robert for a quickie, as

I'd assumed, or was there something far different on her agenda?

With someone else she held 'dear'?

SIXTEEN

This Saturday had seemed even slower than usual and I had the place cleaned, cash register emptied and lights out by 11:30 a.m.

Then I hurried out to the parking lot digging for my keys, intent on getting home to clean up. Across the tracks, I could already see signs of activity. Cars and trucks illegally parked close to the buildings to unload, including…a Ford Escape that looked just like mine.

Probably because it was.

I looked at the empty space where I normally parked my car and closed my purse.

Since Tien and Elaine Riordan had used my SUV to ferry the food, I had to find at least one of them in order to retrieve my keys and drive home. In my head I could hear my son Eric, Benjy the bartender, and even sweet Tien, join in a chorus of 'Well, duh.'

I picked my way across the double row of tracks and mounted the sidewalk that ran along the slaughterhouse. Up close, the building—carved from giant, gray boulders—nearly hunched over on me, and I didn't dare imagine what grisly deeds had been committed inside.

The Ristorante, on the other hand, was cream-colored brick, the sign over the door faded, but still legible. 'Romano's Ristorante—A Place to Meat.'

I looked twice, but yes, it was an 'a'—meat, not

meet. Presumably because of the slaughterhouse. *Not* the theme I'd have struck for the place. Shrugging, I dragged open the heavy door and crossed the threshold.

The foyer of the restaurant was large, with a Dutch-door leading to a coat room on the right side of the hostess stand and restrooms to the left. A menu, mounted on the wall between yellowing reviews from the *Milwaukee Journal* and *Milwaukee Sentinel*, displayed laughably low prices for everything.

Veal, prepared a dozen different ways, was the featured item, both on the menu and in the reviews. You had to give the newspapers five stars for good taste: while extolling the virtues of Romano's fresh veal, the articles never mentioned the poor things were being murdered practically in the next room.

I gave a shiver.

'Can I help you?' a man in jeans and a WTVR T-shirt asked.

'I'm looking for Tien Roman... I mean, Tien? She's in charge of the food service.'

'Oh sure, back there.' He pointed into the dining room and I caught a glimpse of Tien smoothing a table-cloth over a round of six.

'Oh, Maggy, I'm so sorry,' she said when she saw me. 'Here are your car keys.'

'Not a problem,' I said, about to reach for them. 'It's not like you were far away.'

'Still, I planned to return the Escape to our parking lot. I just got caught up.' She swept her free hand around the walls of the room. 'Beautiful venue, isn't it?'

'It is that. But I assume this isn't where—'

'Tien!' a voice called. 'You simply must come see this before the crew hauls everything in.'

Elaine Riordan appeared at a door. 'Oh, Maggy. You, too. It's just that you can't tell anybody.'

I started to say I needed to leave, but Tien was already following her and Tien still had my keys.

Riordan, prancing like a mare on the first day of spring, led us down a corridor lined with doors. The first, and closest to the dining room, was the kitchen. The next two were closed, perhaps leading to offices or storerooms. She finally stopped at a door across the corridor from the last.

'Look at this.' She stepped into the room. 'This is where it all—' her voice dropped—'happened.'

The room, at maybe twenty-feet square, was about the size of the one under the station platform. In fact, it even reminded me of the waiting room. Except, of course, for the bullet holes. Lots and lots of them riddled every wall's paneling.

This time it was Tien's turn to shiver.

'Are you OK?' I asked.

'Yes.' She was standing next to the oblong conference table dominating the room. Two chairs were overturned and there were dark brown stains on the carpet. 'Maggy, do you think they ever tried to clean in here?'

I shook my head. 'Clueless, but I'd guess no.' Maybe it was my imagination, but I could have sworn I saw faint chalk outlines on the floor, the layered 'dust' more like powder to recover latent fingerprints.

Furnished like a corporate boardroom, the resemblance to the waiting area across the tracks was further enhanced by the same carpeting, track-lighting and, in one corner, door—presumably to a small bathroom.

'Maybe we should go,' Tien suggested, her arms clasped across her chest in a self-hug.

'We will,' Riordan said, 'but first, you have to see this.'

She crossed to the bathroom door and as she flung it open I wanted to scream, 'Don't!'

I didn't, of course. Instead, I followed her over and peered in. Except it wasn't a bathroom. 'Just a…closet?'

'Or is it?' Riordan stepped in and slid aside hangers holding what looked like tablecloths. On the wall behind them, was a wood panel. She pushed on it, and it bounced back.

'A secret passage?' Tien had come up behind me.

'To the tunnel?' I was getting caught up in the excitement, despite myself. 'The one that runs under the tracks.'

'Nothing quite so glamorous, I'm afraid,' Elaine Riordan said. 'Though we probably should have known the tunnel could only be legend. The vibration of the trains surely would have wreaked all sorts of havoc on an excavation of that sort.'

Logic. Who needed it? 'So where does this lead?'

'It's a simple escape route through the slaughter-house. Ward thinks the money's probably hidden next door.'

I eyed Gofer Barbie skeptically. 'Maybe, maybe not. But there must be another connection in the kitchen. I mean, how did they get the veal from the slaughter-house into the restaurant?'

She shook her head. 'Oh, Maggy, you're *not* believing those stories about them butchering the carcasses right here, now are you?'

'Well…'

'That was just an old-wives' tale.'

And this not-so-old ex-wife had fallen for it hook, line and sinker.

'C'mon,' Tien said, surprising me as she slipped past my right shoulder to enter the closet. 'Let's go look.'

'At the slaughterhouse?' I realized I was hanging back, like Kate McNamara had when we'd discovered Brigid's body.

And I, ma'am, am no Kate McNamara. If Tien was forging on, given her family's ties to the place, then so was I.

Riordan ducked her head through the door and felt around for a light switch. A click and that buzzing of a fluorescent tube, trying to come to life.

I closed my eyes. What did I think I was going to see? The Ghost of Veal Chops Past?

'What are you doing in there?'

We all jumped.

The same man who had directed me to Tien was standing just outside the closet.

'Just looking around,' I said, backing out. 'There's a secret door in here.'

'No kidding.' He was uncoiling thick wire. 'Except if you tell everyone, it's not going to be so secret anymore.'

'Oh, now, don't you worry,' Riordan said, following Tien out. 'I'm Mr Chitown's assistant?'

'Yeah, well, I'm Mr Chitown's camera operator? Now all of you, get out so I can set up through here.'

And, because he asked so nicely, we did.

BY THE TIME I got back to the Ristorante, it was nearly three thirty. But I was clean, with hair fixed and make-up applied. Wearing a skirt, tank top and a cardigan over them, I looked a little schoolmarmish, and there-fore the better to contrast with my slut dress, currently hidden in a plastic Pick 'n Save bag.

I'd be like the librarian in a movie who pulls off her glasses and lets down her hair to reveal the sex kitten simmering beneath.

Smiling at the thought, I went to help Tien and Jacque. They were assembling buffets, dining tables already filling the center of the room. With the excep-tion of the door leading to the kitchen and hallway, the rear portion had been cordoned off for 'staging'—with apologies to Deirdre Doty, given her dislike of the term—tonight's production.

'Yum,' I said, as I plugged in a giant crock-pot. 'Your clam chowder smells wonderful, Jacque.'

'Only because it eez wonderful.'

I had no reply to that. Over time, I've tried to bond with the man, but the gulf between the level of my kitchen skills and his culinary ego stayed just too deep and too wide.

Members of Deirdre's production crew came stam-peding in, ate efficiently and left as a unit. By the time we'd cleaned up after them, my smartphone read 5:30 and the honored guests would soon be arriving.

But first, a surprise appearance.

'Luc,' I said, going to the door of the dining room. 'I thought you weren't coming.'

'I wasn't, but Sarah insisted.'

Sure enough, my partner air-pushed him from behind. 'Stop grousing. I needed a date, and you're the least annoying unattached male left in the state.'

Tien had followed me out and now gave her father a hug. 'Hey, I thought I was your favorite girl?'

'You are, sweetie,' Luc said, releasing her to look around.

'I think you've been replaced,' I teased Sarah.

'No biggie—I picked him up outside on the sidewalk. Easy come, easy go.'

'So what do you think, Daddy?' Tien was asking. 'Does it look the same as you remembered?'

'Pretty much,' Luc said, moving to the wall leading to the restrooms. 'Look,' he said, pointing to one of five sepia portraits hanging there. 'That's your grandfather.'

As two generations discussed the third via old photos, I tugged Sarah aside by her sleeve. 'You never answered me, you know.'

'About what?'

'Who owns the Ristorante and slaughterhouse?'

'That's public record, but I'm willing to share if you're too lazy to go look it up.'

'Consider me lazy. Now talk.'

'Well, you own the slaughterhouse, you lucky girl.'

'What?'

'OK, along with me and all the other citizens of this fine county.'

Lovely. 'Taken by the assessor for back taxes?'

'Uh-huh.'

I could see it. 'But the Ristorante?'

Sarah nodded toward Luc and Tien at the photo wall. 'The Romano family.'

I glanced around, before I asked in a low voice, 'Do Deirdre and Chitown know?'

'You're worried about the media vultures circling?' Sarah asked. 'A condition of allowing our current "production crew" in was that they leave Luc and Tien "utterly, completely, and totally" alone.'

'Nicely done,' I said. 'And at your insistence?'

'You're welcome.' Sarah scanned the long dark-wood counter that lined one wall and frowned. 'What, no open bar?'

'No bar open, period,' I said. 'Apparently Chitown would like the observers sober until we get to the celebration at Sapphire.'

'That seems a little short-sighted,' Sarah said. 'What if Chitown doesn't find his treasure? The anticlimax could seriously deep-six the—' finger quotes— '"celebration".'

I hoped Sarah hadn't started celebrating a little early herself. 'Are you OK?'

'Fine. Over the last five days, my only remaining employee *and* my biggest competition have been murdered, and I think your boyfriend still has me as his primo suspect.'

'But are you—'

'OK? Yeah. I doubled all my meds. That OK with you?'

Yikes. 'Sure, of course.' I hesitated before I said, 'If it makes you feel any better, Pavlik said that Gabriella was shot with a smaller gun than yours.'

'Goody. That must be why they were looking for a .22-caliber anything when they came by with their search warrant this morning.'

'They didn't!'

'They did.'

'When?'

'Oddly enough, right before I upped my meds. Now, though, you'd better get that food out.' She hitchhiked a thumb over her shoulder. 'The guests are arriving.'

Sure enough, Art Jenada and Kate McNamara had just entered the restaurant, Art making a left to the men's room, Kate continuing on into the dining area.

I turned tail and hurried back to the kitchen to help Jacque move things along, leaving Tien and her father still studying their family photos.

'What eez that?' Jacque demanded, as I went to pick up a plate with magical aromas coming off something breaded.

'Umm, crab cakes?' I figured this to be a pop quiz, like when I stopped by to pick up snapper at Jacque's fish counter and he interrogated me on how I was going to prepare it.

'No, no, no. Not *that*,' he said imperiously. '*That!*'

Jacque was pointing toward the palm of my right hand. 'Oh—just a rash. I must have touched a plant I'm allergic—'

'Then you will *not* touch my food.' He whisked the plate from my hand.

'It's not poison ivy or something I could spread,' I protested, 'just…contact dermatitis or something.' Something being the operative word.

But Jacque was making a show of transferring the miniature crab cakes to another, presumably untainted, platter. 'You will put on gloves or you will go.'

As I deliberated, Tien entered, with Luc trailing. 'Did you cut yourself, Maggy?'

'No, I just have this.' I showed her.

'Eeuuw, nasty. Does it itch?'

'A little,' I admitted.

'You go on, Maggy,' Luc said. 'I'll help out here.' He, too, seemed creeped out by my rash.

I left the kitchen, feeling a mite hurt and muttering under my breath. 'It's not like I have an open sore.'

'Excuse me?' Deirdre Doty was to the right of the door, watching as a technician dragged heavy cables through the dining area like a harnessed farm horse clearing felled trees. At the back of the room, carpenters were, not surprisingly, hammering and nailing.

'Nothing,' I said, pulling the cuffs of my cardigan down over my hands. 'How are things going?'

'Organized chaos, but that's to be expected at this point of the process and we'll weather it eventually.' Doty scanned the room. 'Have you seen Ward?'

'No, I—'

'Oh, there they are.'

The producer left me to gather up Chitown and Elaine Riordan, who'd just come in the front door. Elaine was laden with her huge shoulder bag and a big antique typewriter. Chitown was carrying nothing but himself, though with smug aplomb.

The next people to arrive were a couple of suits and then our Brookhills County district attorney and...

'Jane?'

Jane Smith pivoted. 'Maggy, how good to see you.'

Wearing a jersey wrap dress, she looked considerably more together than she had been the last time I'd seen her. Namely, being questioned by a sheriff's deputy about Gabriella Atherton's death and, subsequently, ducking out of MaryAnne's backyard before the neighbor/homeowner could see her.

I'd thought it odd at the time, and now was my chance to ask. I beckoned Smith aside and she reluctantly released her escort's arm and followed me.

'You and the DA are an item?' I asked.

'Perhaps,' Smith said, her tone telling me that, though we had shared a magical moment over a body, I was still the shopkeeper and she the Barbie.

'Well, good for you,' I said, slapping her on the back. 'Now tell me, why did you make a beeline out of Mary-Anne's yard? Didn't want her to know you'd been nosing around?'

'Of course not.' Smith's chin trembled. 'I was being a good neighbor. I saw activity in her yard when I knew she wasn't home and went to investigate.'

Now Smith's tone projected, 'That's my story and I'm sticking to it.'

'So why'd you run, then, instead of offering to help said neighbor?'

'I didn't want to add to MaryAnne's burden. She had enough on her hands with the open house and… Gabriella's body and all.'

I just looked at Smith.

'All right, fine.' A panicky glance toward the DA, who didn't even appear to notice Smith was no longer at his side. 'It was something she'd said. I…needed to think.'

'Something Gabriella Atherton said?'

Smith pitched her voice so low I could barely hear

the words. 'No, what *MaryAnne* said as I was approaching all of you.'

'OK, Jane. Give.' I'd been there, and I sure didn't remember anything unusual. Except for the body in the pool, of course.

Smith scooted even closer to whisper in my ear. 'MaryAnne asked what Gabriella had been doing there.'

'Yeah, so?'

'But don't you see? MaryAnne already *knew*. When Gabriella left your shop, she said it was...'

'To meet with a client, or so you told Sarah and me.'

A heavy sigh. 'I was trying to be circumspect. I didn't know MaryAnne was going to deny it.'

Wait a minute. 'Are you saying *MaryAnne* was that client?'

Finally a smile. 'Good for you, Maggy.' Jane Smith slapped me on my back, rather vengefully, I thought, and rejoined her quasi-date.

SEVENTEEN

NOW I NEEDED to digest what Jane Smith had just told me, but it didn't look like I would have the opportunity any time soon. People needed to be fed and, if I shouldn't touch the food, at least I could bus dirty dishes from the tables.

Which I'm sure didn't help my 'shopkeeper' status, I thought as I took Smith's plate, still nearly full. Honest to God, did these Barbies eat anything?

Two uniformed sheriff's deputies were seated at one table finishing up their meals, but it was getting close to showtime and still no sign of our sheriff himself.

Just as I had that thought, my cell rang. Caller ID told me what I needed to know. 'Pavlik?'

'Listen, Maggy, I'm sorry, but I'm not going to be able to make it tonight.'

My heart dropped. 'You mean for the show, right? You'll be at Sapphire afterwards?'

'Neither. With another murder, I need to be on-scene.'

'But…a couple of your deputies have already arrived.'

'Because I sent them to represent the department. I just don't think I should be out partying when people are dying on my watch.'

Much as I didn't want to understand, I did. Pavlik

was absolutely right. He shouldn't be here. Even more so, for public relations reasons he shouldn't be *seen* here.

That didn't stop me from being disappointed, though.

'I'll miss you,' I said softly. I heard my voice crack, like that fourteen-year-old of yore.

'Maggy?' There was astonishment in his voice. 'Are you crying?'

'No.' I turned toward the wall of the dining room and tented my forehead against it.

'Then why does your voice sound funny?'

'Bad connection.' I swallowed. 'Umm, see you tomorrow?'

'Assuming I don't see you at a crime scene before then.'

By six forty-five, we, the live audience, were seated in folding chairs facing the stage I'd seen being built. The structure would likely look good on camera, but I knew it to be plywood and the plants plastic. A battered desk like something out of *The Untouchables* was positioned in the center, a rolling office chair behind it.

A bare bones 'guest' chair squatted beside the desk, and the manual typewriter Elaine Riordan had been carrying slumped on the writing service.

'Hot damn, is that an Underwood?' Sarah, sitting to my right, intoned the word like a car nut might the marque Stutz Bearcat. She sighed nostalgically. 'My mother had one of those.'

My partner had saved front row seats for Tien, Luc, Jacque and me, since we'd needed to put the food away and clean up after everyone was finally done eating.

Unfortunately, there were two more chairs in the row, and Kate McNamara took the one next to me as I welcomed our catering crew.

Kate's greeting? 'Maggy, shush!'

Art was sitting beside Kate, Elaine Riordan leaning down to speak with him. He looked surprised, then got up and moved to the row behind us.

'I'm sorry,' Riordan said, settling into Art's former seat. 'But I need to be right here so I can assist onstage if needed. There really should have been a sign on this particular chair.'

'Reserved for the lead go-fer?' Kate hissed to me from the corner of her mouth.

My, my. I sensed a sore spot.

I smiled. 'Haven't seen much of you lately, Kate. I thought Ward and you were like this.' I crossed two fingers tightly.

'I'm not sure where you got that idea,' she said stiffly. 'I was simply showing him around. Though Ward and I do have such similar backgrounds it's almost uncanny.'

'Yeah. TV careers that crashed and burned,' Sarah said into the other ear.

'I'm sure you do,' I said smoothly to Kate. 'He's quite the charmer, isn't he?'

She threw me a startled look as Deirdre Doty stepped onto the stage, holding a sheaf of two-foot-square placards. She was dressed in a pair of dark-wash trouser jeans and a contrasting lace cami under a short, fitted jacket.

'Thank you all for coming. I'm Deirdre Doty, Ward Chitown's producer. Ward has asked me to brief you before we start.

'As you know, this is a live show. We break for commercials, but other than that, we just keep going. We will be using at least two other locations, so please be ready to move as quickly and as orderly as possible. Ward also asks that you remain absolutely quiet, except when I signal you for an appropriate reaction.'

From her sheaf, she raised a sign that read: 'APPLAUSE!'

Elaine Riordan clapped wildly and, getting the idea, we did the same, though barely politely.

The next sign said: 'SURPRISE!'

Elaine gasped. Ditto for us, me to swallow…

'LAUGHTER!'

Where the shepherdess led, the flock again followed.

'Good, good. You get the idea,' Doty said with a little grin. 'But don't go overboard. Just let your natural reactions shine through.'

'Yeah, right,' Sarah said. 'I feel like I'm in the studio audience for an *I Love Lucy* episode. Any minute now, Ricky's going to sashay out from the wings with his conga drum.'

As if cued, Ward Chitown strode onto the stage in a well-cut suit. Even without Doty's flash card, we onlookers applauded.

'Thank you so much, Deirdre. And my personal welcome to all our Brookhills friends. We wanted to repay your kindness *to* us and your patience *with* us, by including you here tonight to witness…history.'

Another swell of applause, though maybe twelve people were more a gaggle than a swell.

'We're live in thirty seconds,' Doty said loudly. She'd added a headset to her ensemble. 'Positions, everybody.'

Ward Chitown hitched his butt onto the edge of the desk, facing us and the camera in casual candor.

'Ward, two inches left,' Doty directed. 'We want to get the typewriter.'

'That's my antique Underwood,' Elaine Riordan chirped. 'Isn't this exciting?'

'Electrifying,' Sarah muttered. Then: 'Oh, I'm sorry. It's a manual.'

Lame typewriter jokes, the inevitable consequence of doubling one's medication.

'Quiet on the set!' Deirdre Doty held up one hand, fingers extended toward snapping to her palm in a countdown. 'We're live in five, four, three, two...' She pointed the last finger at the star himself.

'Good evening, America! I'm Ward Chitown and I'm here to reveal, with you—' he pointed at the camera lens—'the historic, secret treasure of... Romano's Raid.'

The APPLAUSE! placard went up. We clapped and, as Doty signaled to keep it rolling, even cheered a bit.

Chitown held up his hands as modest, dual stop signs. 'Thank you, thank you. Now, let me tell you how tonight will unfold. Currently, we are broadcasting live from the town of Brookhills, Wisconsin.

'Today, Brookhills is still a small town, but for decades it has been an affluent one as well. Its citizens shop and play tennis, do lunch and...'

Drink coffee, I willed him to say.

'...attend theater. Many of the people who live here work in the city of Milwaukee, commuting there by car or the new commuter-rail line which was christened just last month.

'But Brookhills has a long-concealed seamier side, as well. This room we're in…' Chitown waved majestically to a camera operator, who panned one wall toward the entrance, careful to keep 'we' the audience out of the frame.

I looked down at the Uncommon Grounds Styrofoam cup in my hand. Fat lot of good it was going to do our business, unless I threw it at Chitown on stage.

'…is the quaint main dining room of Romano's Ristorante, shuttered for more than thirty-five years. A beautiful setting as I believe we all can agree.' A drop in Chitown's voice from tenor to baritone. 'But also one shadowed by a past both dark and deep. A heritage that involved the Mafia and its nefarious schemes. A situation that inexorably put eight men—four agents of the Federal Bureau of Investigation, or FBI, and four gangsters—on a deadly collision course.'

Now Chitown's voice descended from baritone to bass. 'A shoot-out between the forces of good and evil. Only two men survived. One?' Hand reverently pressed to heart. 'My father, Samuel Chitown, the FBI agent in charge of the raid.'

A pause. I had to admit, Chitown had a gift for drama. Or, at least, melodrama.

'Who, though, you might ask, was the other man? His name was Antonio Solari and he was the consigliere, the lawyer-cum-confidential-advisor, of the Chicago Outfit that controlled this part of the Mafia realm.

'Solari had been dispatched to Brookhills in order that he might maintain the uneasy peace between the Midwest crime families as they divided cash skimmed from their Las Vegas casinos. But legend tells us that it was not the peace that Solari kept…' Another pregnant pause. 'But rather…the loot.'

Chitown slid his rump off the desk edge and started to pace laterally, stage-right to stage-left and back again, the camera lens following him. 'Over a million dollars in 1974 money, though no one knows the exact amount for sure, except the man who made off with it.

'Our only true certainty? When the smoke cleared in the back room of this restaurant located, ironically, next to a slaughterhouse and across the tracks from the train depot, six men lay dead and the skimmed cash was…gone.'

Now Chitown stopped and engaged the camera straight on, legs planted, eyes blazing. 'Or was it?'

The APPLAUSE! sign went up.

'And…we're…out!' Deirdre Doty pronounced.

Elaine Riordan hopped up and brought a cup of water to Chitown.

'Leave it on the desk,' I chanted as a mantra. 'Leave it on the desk.'

Sarah asked, 'Are you all right?'

I nodded toward the cup, still in Chitown's hand. 'It has our logo on the side.'

'Oh, yeah. Smart, Maggy.'

What did she think? I got to where I was now—the nearly broke co-owner of a struggling coffeehouse—being stupid?

Hell, yes. Let me count the ways.

'All right. Positions again, everybody.' Deirdre once more straightening her fingers. 'And we're live in…'

And so it went.

The next segment included shadowy footage of the

depot and The Mob's Waiting Room, presumably a
play on 'God's Waiting Room'. Partway through, Sarah
started to snore. I elbowed her.

'Wha'?'

Deirdre Doty's eyes shot darts.

Chitown was talking. Still. '…agents crept through
this room, perhaps signaling any innocent bystanders
to leave. Sadly, perhaps even tragically, the restaurant's
owner, Joseph Romano, was killed in the crossfire.'
He shook his head. '*Probably* just collateral damage.'

I glanced over at Luc and Tien. Luc was looking
straight ahead, a tear sliding down his cheek but his jaw
clenched, I assumed from Chitown's smarmy ambigu-
ity about Father Romano's possible involvement on the
Mafia's side of the raid. Tien squeezed her father's hand.

'When we come back live again, we'll bring you
into the infamous boardroom where the actual carnage
took place.'

'Oh, good,' Sarah said, after Doty signaled we were
in commercial. 'Carnage.'

'Oh, good,' I parroted, standing up a bit stiffly. 'We
get to move. C'mon.'

The next segment took place, as promised, in the
boardroom. There was just enough space for us, the
unwashed audience, to stand out of camera range. Chitown's on-camera narrative seemed mostly a rehash
of what already had been said, the only development
vaguely interesting being Chitown's revelation of that
secret panel in the back of the closet.

Since I already knew about it, though, yesteryear's
news was a bit of a snooze.

Besides, I was still smarting from the fact there'd

been no mention of Uncommon Grounds during the footage they'd taped at the depot. *'Deirdre and Ward want you to get as much product-placement value as possible.'* My ass.

Sarah, though, seemed to have perked up by the time we went to another commercial break. 'A secret door. Maybe it's to the tunnel running under the tracks.'

'Nah,' I said. 'No such luck. It leads to the slaughterhouse. They would sneak out through there and then cross the tracks to hang out in *our* secret room until the train came.'

'That's a little low-tech. How do you know?'

'Elaine showed Tien and me this morning.'

Doty was doing another countdown.

Sarah groaned. 'So…no tunnel?'

I shook my head.

'MOVE QUICKLY, PLEASE.' Deirdre Doty again—or maybe still: I was becoming numbed to the passage of time— herded us into the slaughterhouse. We were noticeably losing discipline as a flock in the absence of a Border collie nipping at our heels.

I might be a partial owner, according to Sarah, but I did *not* want to go into the slaughterhouse.

Especially now, when the place appeared to be lit up like a blood-soaked Christmas tree. God knows, I'd by then seen plenty of blood and plenty of bodies, but there was something just so wrong about a place… *dedicated* to killing.

'This is a House of Execution, partner,' I said to Sarah, 'only its victims were one-hundred-percent innocent. And with such gentle, trusting eyes.' I sniffled.

Sarah smacked her lips. 'And such nice rib-eyes, especially on the grill over mesquite-flavored briquettes, with—'

'I'll wait here,' I said, hanging back.

'Not when you're blocking the door,' Sarah said, putting both palms on my back and shoving.

I stumbled through, nearly running into a concrete-block pillar inside the door. I caught myself just in time, jamming my wrist against the concrete. Reflexively, I pulled back, imagining stickiness in what was likely a blood splatter more than thirty years old and drier than dust.

Stepping around the pillar, we the audience found ourselves in a large room with walls of concrete block, like the pillar. Nearly every inch of the expansive floor was stained varying shades of dark brown. There were huge drains beneath our feet, the nearest beginning about a shoe-length away from me. A faded, cracked hose was coiled in one corner. In another, a wooden column stood, and hanging on that...

'Oh, my God,' I said, putting the back of my hand up to my mouth. 'Meat hooks?'

'What in the world is wrong?' Sarah said. 'It's not like you don't enjoy a nice burger.'

'Not anymore,' I said. Our group was being gathered into one area, all of us standing, and most with arms folded across our chests. Primordial instinct, Eric would say. Assuming a defensive posture for protection against the...unknown.

'All right, people. Quiet, please,' Deirdre Doty ordered again, though no one was whispering, much less speaking aloud. 'We're live in five, four...'

'And now we've reached our...*final* destination,' Ward Chitown intoned. 'The slaughterhouse, next door to the restaurant. But more than mere cattle and veal calves died here. My father believed that known Mafia hitmen also brought their...human victims to this killing floor.

'Imagine: it would have been so easy.' His hand swept toward the hose. 'A pressurized water source to wash down the blood, with drains in the floor to carry away the gruesome cocktail into city sewers. Then, spread a little bleach and—' he shrugged—'would anyone even know the difference?

'This was also where Antonio Solari ran, bleeding from gunshot wounds and desperately clutching a grocery bag that held the cash skimmed from the casinos. Everyone, including my own father, believed he had escaped with more than a million dollars. The only winner in a losing game.'

Chitown approached the camera slowly, shaking his index finger even more so, like a metronome. 'Because make no mistake about it. No one really won that day. Three wives buried their FBI-agent husbands and seven children grew up without their FBI fathers.'

I saw Tien put an arm around Luc and lay her head on his shoulder.

'Even Antonio Solari was not a winner, eventually. Nor even a survivor. Now, nearly forty years later, I'm here to tell you that Solari himself died that day. His body was found near the Illinois state line, not identified until just recently, thanks to DNA testing. Police photographs of the then John Doe show that he was fully clothed and had a gunshot wound to the leg, one that caused Solari to bleed out before he could make it from the train station in Kenosha, Wisconsin, to his childhood home nearby.'

Chitown sighed deeply, closing his eyes. 'But…whatever happened to the money?'

Reluctantly, I had to admit I was riveted by his performance. I wanted to scream, 'Yeah, where is it?'

'Yeah, where is it?' Sarah yelled for both of us.

My evil twin—let her take the heat. But this time, neither Deirdre nor Kate displayed the 'shush' signal.

'I'll tell you where it is,' Chitown said, nodding affably at the outburst. 'And, I will tell you…now.'

'What do you bet we go to a commercial?' Sarah whispered to me.

But Chitown was walking toward us. He knelt by the drain at the base of the pillar I'd barged into and he held out his palm, upward and open. Like a surgical nurse, Deirdre Doty slapped a yellow-handled screwdriver into it.

'Watch carefully,' Chitown called and we all shuffled forward. The hell with Deirdre and her 'Stay out of the shot' or 'Keep quiet'. We wanted to see.

And see we did.

Chitown used the screwdriver to pry up an edge of the drain grate. Not quite able to keep the filthy iron away from his designer suit, he rolled the grate aside. Then, barehanded, Chitown reached down into the drain, eventually having to bellyflop onto the equally filthy floor, his arm disappearing to the shoulder, his facial features twisting grotesquely from the strain of… 'No good. Dammit!' He pounded his other fist against the floor, still apparently unable to dip deeply enough.

He again picked up the screwdriver, gripped it as an extension of his hand and plunged both back into the hole.

Everybody—yes, including me—held our breath until…finally…an inch at a time, Ward Chitown's arm began craning upward, ever upward. And, when that screwdriver finally reappeared, a worn, plastic grocery bag dangled precariously at its tip, corners of green currency poking out from a partial tear in the bag's bottom.

EIGHTEEN

'AMAZING,' I SAID to Sarah, as Ward Chitown signed off and turned the money over to the two men in business suits I'd seen arriving earlier.

Apparently, they were certified public accountants, now counting the loot instead of tallying votes for the Oscars.

'What's amazing? That Chitown didn't come up empty *a la* Geraldo?'

'Exactly.'

'Ward knew the money was down there,' Elaine Riordan said from beside us and nearly bursting with pent-up excitement. 'He and Deirdre found it when they scouted the slaughterhouse on Monday, but told no one, not even *me*, until now.'

The woman giggled and ran off.

'Balls of steel,' Sarah said.

I looked at her.

'I mean to leave the cash there for the better part of a week. What if one of our even more amateurish treasure hunters had found it?'

'After all these years?' I said. 'Besides, our other amateurs were too busy digging holes in our lawn.'

'True. I wonder if Chitown'd have been so sanguine about leaving it if he'd realized the bag was ripped and might be leaking c-notes.'

I was watching the suits do their count. The bills looked damp and…oh, was that dark splotch another bloodstain?

Ugh. The 'ambience' was closing in on me, making my stomach turn queasy. 'How about we go back into the Ristorante?'

'Sure, but I can't stay. I have to run home and change for the party.'

'You're dressing up?' It was unusual to see Sarah in anything beyond her jackets and trousers. I'd seen her legs in a tennis skirt once, but that had been an aberration. And a little frightening.

She nodded toward my sensible outfit. 'You're wearing that?'

Might as well, given that Pavlik wouldn't be there. But that was the fourteen-year-old talking again. 'I have a change of clothes in the car. I'll get dressed in the restaurant ladies' room and meet you at Sapphire.'

I followed Sarah out of the closet and into the boardroom. 'And, given that—' I poked my thumb toward the hubbub still going on around the money behind us—'I think it's going to be quite the party.'

The dining room of the restaurant was a hive of activity. Cables were being recoiled and cameras packed up now that the live production—at least at this location—had ended. But at the same time, the local news operations began making their way into the Ristorante.

'The other stations must have been watching,' I said, recognizing an on-air reporter with the Milwaukee CBS affiliate as he blasted by me. 'Didn't take them long to get here.'

'Oh, they had their trucks lined up along the road

right outside,' Elaine Riordan said smugly. The woman seemed to be everywhere. Right now, she was lifting her dinosaur typewriter off the desk so workmen could move the old desk and dismantle the makeshift stage.

'Most excitement Brookhills has seen in a while,' Sarah said, raising her hand. 'Catch you later.'

As she left, I looked around. 'Anything I can help you with, Elaine?'

'Oh, that's so nice of you, Maggy. You don't mind?'

'Not at all. I need to change for the party, but I have my things with me and it's probably going to be at least an hour before anyone gets over to Sapphire anyway.'

'I'm sure.' Riordan strained to lovingly lower the Underwood onto the floor next to her leather handbag which probably weighed somewhere close to a side of beef.

Which reminded me, unfortunately, of the slaughterhouse.

As I swallowed back another wave of queasiness, Riordan straightened. 'What an exciting night, Maggy. I'm so happy to be part of it.'

'Well, happiness agrees with you.' It was true. The woman was practically glowing.

Now she blushed. 'I have to tell you, I feel better right now than I have in weeks.'

'Had you been ill?' Or depressed, I was thinking. I gestured for her to join me in folding up the front row of chairs.

'I really feared so,' Riordan said, sitting down instead of helping. 'My weight has dropped and I have the most horrible headaches sometimes.'

MaryAnne Williams had mentioned the weight loss,

though if I'd noticed at all—never a sure bet—I'd have attributed it to Barbies just being Barbies. Never thin enough or rich enough. 'Have you been to a doctor?'

'No.' Another blush, but a different 'shade' than the happy one. 'With the divorce and all, health insurance has been a problem.'

'You know it's possible that… I'm not saying your symptoms are psychosomatic, but I was quite depressed after my divorce.'

'Really, Maggy?' Riordan studied my face. 'I had no idea.'

'Hey, Elaine, we're women. We've learned how to be good at hiding things and just soldiering on.'

She was nodding. 'You're so right. And…well, I honestly hadn't considered the possibility that depression might be the reason I was feeling so awful physically.'

'But you just told me you're better now?'

'So much better,' Riordan said, holding her hands palm-up. 'It's like a great weight has been lifted from these shoulders.'

'Being active makes a huge difference,' I agreed. 'Throwing yourself into new projects. I mean, so long as you don't do something stupid.'

Like quitting your corporate PR job and opening a coffeehouse.

'That's exactly it, Maggy. These past couple of weeks, I have taken control of my life again. It's made all the difference in the world.'

'In the game', as MaryAnne had put it.

I patted Elaine on one now-lighter shoulder. 'Being part of something unusual like this—' I pointed to the knot of reporters gathered around Ward Chitown, now holding court just outside the board room—'has to be a real upper.'

Hell, even I was stoked, despite having my red dress in the car but no Pavlik to see it.

'Holding one's head high and looking forward instead of backwards.' Riordan rose. 'I feel empowered, even reborn.'

I laughed and stood, too. 'We'd better stop there or we'll break into a chorus of "I Am Woman".'

Riordan laughed as well, then retrieved her handbag. 'God bless that Helen Reddy? She gave us an anthem for the ages.'

'For *all* our ages. Can I at least give you a hand with that?'

Riordan had the strap of her big purse resting in the saddle of her left shoulder, but each time she leaned down to pick up the typewriter, her bag slipped down as well, landing with an audible 'clunk' on top of the ancient Underwood. 'I...just can't seem...'

I gently nudged Riordan aside and scooped up the typewriter. No mean feat, either. The thing had to weigh nearly fifty pounds. 'Where to, Elaine?' I asked, trying not to gasp or whimper.

'To my car, if that's not too far?'

'Of course not,' I lied.

Riordan led our way out the front door of the restaurant. Street parking had been prohibited for the night—unless, of course, you were a broadcast media company with enough bucks to keep a driver behind the steering wheel so a given vehicle was never really 'parked'.

I followed her across Junction Road to a public lot

used during the day by Kate McNamara's newspaper, *The Observer*. Riordan's little beige car was parked just an aisle away from my Escape. I'd drop off the type-writer, grab the bag with my dress and change in the restroom.

Assuming I even made it to her car. Damn, but the Underwood was heavy. And awkward to carry. I shifted the thing, letting the bottom bite into other sections of my palms. *So* much better. And the temporary pain even made the persistent itching of my rash-covered hand recede from conscious sensation.

Chitown should be the one with the itchy palm. He'd found the long-lost money, though the pursuit of that particular rainbow—leading to a resurrected television career—might prove more lucrative than the proverbial pot of gold itself. Good thing, because given the back taxes owed on the slaughterhouse, I wasn't sure Chi-town would see a cent of the 'treasure' anyway.

'Oh, Maggy. Thank you so much.' Elaine was snif-fling as she unlocked the trunk of her little car.

'Happy to help. Are you sure you don't have aller-gies?' I asked, as I hefted the typewriter up and over the lip of her trunk. 'They can cause headaches, you know.'

Riordan's signature afghan was folded neatly in one corner of the trunk and as I settled the Underwood in, the luggage compartment was nearly full. Her big hand-bag—Kleenex box and all—would have to go into the cabin of the car itself. And, given the presumed weight of the leather tote, it probably should have an airbag of its own.

'You're a really good person, Maggy, and I'm not talking about just carrying the typewriter. I enjoyed our talk.' She slung her handbag onto her left shoulder and hugged me in an awkward way, like she didn't engage in the gesture very often.

Holy shit, I thought. Maybe MaryAnne was right. I *am* a mensch.

Nah.

'You might want to put something around the typewriter to protect it,' I said. 'If an antique Underwood really is worth something, you wouldn't want it getting bounced around.'

I picked up the only other thing in her trunk—the afghan—and shook it out of the plastic bag it had been stowed in to check for 'padding' capacity. Happily, no ball of yarn fell out.

'Oh, I'm sure it'll be fine as it is,' Riordan said, reaching for her handiwork.

She grabbed one edge and the thing stretched to its full length, displaying a roughly circular hole larger than I thought the loose crochet could account for.

'Uh-oh,' I said, fingering it delicately. 'You have a tear here or maybe you just missed a stitch.' Or three, given the size of the hole.

I rubbed my thumb and forefinger together. In the illumination of the overhead street lights, I could see a trace of black and the acrylic yarn felt melted and crusted around the edges of the circle, like someone held a cigarette to it.

'Maggy, thanks ever so much for your concern, but it's truly nothing,' Riordan said. 'Just a burn. Once I wash the afghan and mend it you'll barely notice.'

I had my doubts, but that *was* the nice thing about synthetics. They do launder well. I let my end of her afghan go.

Only my fingers came away…sticky?

NINETEEN

ASTONISHING HOW MANY things can flash through your mind in no more than an instant.

For example, the zigzag pattern of the crocheted afghan and the irregular pattern of stippling on the side of Gabriella Atherton's face.

The easy-care fabric that, given Elaine Riordan's all-consuming responsibilities since yesterday, hadn't been washed and therefore had to be stashed in the trunk of her car.

And then there was Gabriella Atherton herself, the woman Riordan had caught in her own marital bed with her then-husband, Robert.

The woman who was about to marry that now exhusband, leaving Riordan with almost nothing, not even health insurance.

And the other women? They were the trees that hid the forest. Or vice versa. Either way, 'Gabriella was the real victim.'

Riordan had turned away to bundle the afghan into her trunk and it was only when she pivoted back that I realized I'd said the last aloud.

'Gabriella, a victim? It's women like you and me who are the "real victims" of the Gabriellas of this world, Maggy. And I was damned if I was going to let her marry my Robert.' Riordan clutched her handbag like it was the man she couldn't let go.

'But what difference would it make whether they married or not? The damage has been done. You and Robert are divorced.'

'Only because of her,' Riordan said. 'You see, with Gabriella out of the way, Robert will come back to me. He and I will have a second wedding. And honeymoon.' A weird smile creased her mouth. 'Especially when I tell him I'm sick, as anyone can plainly see.'

Depended on what you meant by 'sick'. I shrugged. 'And are you?'

'Sick? I told you.' Riordan slammed down her trunk lid, but it bounced right back up. 'I lost weight. My hair even started to fall out and I was getting headaches. I knew I had cancer and I was going to die. I had no insurance.'

I remembered that Robert had said his ex texted him, asking about COBRA coverage from his employer. Which she'd let lapse, given the crushing expense of each premium. 'Did you go to a doctor?'

'No.' Riordan was shouting now. 'I *told* you: I don't have insurance. If I'd been diagnosed, even Robert's company insurance policy might not have taken me back.'

Pre-existing condition. God help her—and us— she was probably right on that point. 'Please don't tell me you took four innocent lives just to get *insurance* again?'

'Four...?' Elaine shook her head, violently. 'I killed one guilty home-breaker to get my *life* back again.'

Gabriella, I could see. Elaine Riordan had a vendetta against her.

Brigid, who knew? The woman reportedly came on to anybody with money and a pulse. Maybe that included Robert Riordan.

But…'Elaine, did you even know the first two women?'

'Of course. They were horrible to me. Ridiculed me, laughed at me not just behind my back, but to my face. You can ask anyone.'

Like Sarah, who had said Riordan was an embarrassment even to the Broker Barbies. But that didn't mean they should be shot, execution-style, like a professional killer would the objects of his or her contracts.

I said, 'So they had to die, too?'

A look I'd never seen before crossed Elaine's face. I couldn't even call it an expression, because it 'expressed' nothing. Even her eyes showed no emotion, just two glazed buttons, displaying depth but not emotion. 'Better them than me, Maggy.'

A shiver rippled up my spine. 'How did you get Gabriella to MaryAnne's?'

'"Where are you, honey?"' Riordan's voice was suddenly stronger, the Southern lilt more pronounced. A perfect mimic of MaryAnne. '"I've changed my mind on listing the house. Honey, can you come right on over?"'

The cellphone call Atherton had received in Uncommon Grounds, the one with the 'poor connection'. That explained why Gabriella told Jane Smith her new client was MaryAnne. Atherton genuinely believed that's who she was going to meet.

'MaryAnne told me you stayed with her for a while after your divorce. You would have had a key to Mary-Anne's house.'

A cackling laugh. 'I even tried to give it back, but she is just such a generous person? She insisted I keep it, just in case.'

'And you repaid her kindness by killing a person in her swimming pool and leaving the gate open to hide the fact the killer had a key?'

'No, Maggy. Not a "person". Gabriella Atherton. Home-breaker...slut!'

The red 'slut' dress in my own car flashed through my brain.

'Besides—' Riordan shrugging now—'MaryAnne didn't have to actually *deal* with the mess. I mean, she *does* have a pool boy.'

A glimpse of the pre-divorce Elaine Riordan. When she had her pride and enough money to indulge it.

Riordan used the pause after 'pool boy' to dip into her massive purse.

I, on the other hand, took advantage of the brief pause to turn away.

And run. I'd make it an all-out, fist-pumping...

But I stumbled right out of the box, toe catching heel, putting me down in a heap on the parking lot's gravel.

I swiveled my head. In her right hand, Riordan held a little gun, its barrel not more than a couple of inches long.

'Let me...' My voice quavered. 'Let me guess, Elaine. A twenty-two caliber?'

She nodded. 'Manufacturer, Beretta. Model, Bobcat.

The perfect self-defense weapon? Which, of course, is what I was doing.'

The woman was a sociopath. Nothing mattered but her goal, obstacles in the way toward it be damned.

God knows I could identify with that, but... I had people whose well-being I put before mine. Most important of all, my son Eric.

Riordan waggled her gun. 'Now get to your feet. Slowly.'

I complied, less than three feet separating us. Riordan put her free left hand on the still-raised trunk lid. 'Now get into the car. We're going for a ride.'

There was no way I was going anywhere with this woman. 'Don't you want to take the afghan out before you close the trunk? That way you can throw it over my head before you shoot me through the temple, like you must have done with the others.'

Riordan cocked her head to the side. 'Why, Maggy. That is such a *fine* idea. I admit it does help a little lady like me to get the drop on someone. That, and I'm afraid I'm such an embarrassment when I go digging through my bag, it's not unusual for people to turn away.'

Like Sarah had, when Riordan's yarn made a run for it just before we discovered Brigid Ferndale's body.

In contrast, Elaine managed to keep her eye on me just fine as she reached down for the afghan with her left hand. The aforementioned bag, though, slipped off her shoulder as it had earlier when she'd tried to pick up the typewriter. Weight thrown forward, she instinctively put her gun hand out to steady herself on the typewriter.

That's when I jumped as high as I could, spread my hands, and devoted every ounce of me to slamming the trunk lid closed.

TWENTY

THE DAMN THING came right back up again, but this time because it had bounced off Elaine Riordan's right forearm.

So I slammed the lid down thrice more, my lungs screaming bloody murder the whole time.

I still don't remember whether Riordan did the same.

Ironically, it was Kate McNamara and her media brethren who first came to my aid.

Not to restrain Riordan, mind you, but rather to photograph every angle of my wrestling the lightweight, bone-fractured Barbie to the ground and then sitting on her—literally—until real help arrived in the form of the two sheriff's deputies, Pavlik's representatives, who had still been inside the slaughterhouse.

They took one look at me, and the older brought out a cellphone. He, like me, had Pavlik on speed-dial.

'Good job,' said the sheriff an hour later as we sat side-by-side on the rear hatch of my open Escape, a safe distance away from the insatiable hordes of media—both print *and* broadcast now—who had descended on the area.

Or who, like Kate, thanks to her undeserved great Luck of the Irish, was already there.

'Good job?' I repeated. 'Please Pavlik, know this is *one* fight I did not go looking for.'

He reached up and pushed an errant lock of hair behind my ear. 'Since you're all right, I'll admit that in this case I'm glad you were involved. Elaine Riordan was not on our radar screen and she should have been.'

'Because she was the ex-wife of Gabriella Atherton's fiancé? You would have gotten to her eventually. Thing is, Elaine seemed like such a timid little thing.'

'Those are the people you have to watch out for. The ones who bottle things up until they explode, taking everybody in the vicinity with them.'

'I guess.' I leaned against him. 'Don't suppose you want to come to the party now, huh? I mean, since your homicide cases are all closed.'

'I take your point, but I still think it would be poor form.' Pavlik massaged my shoulder. 'I do think you should go, though.'

'Without you, I'm not sure I'm up for it.'

'Of course you are.' He turned me toward him, hands on both shoulders now. 'Everyone who is anyone—except me, of course—will be there and you just cleared a string of homicides, missy. You deserve to enjoy your evening.'

'Missy?' I gave him a quick kiss. 'Well… Sarah is meeting me there and I'd hate to disappoint her. Besides—' I pointed to the balled-up Pick 'n Save bag next to the Escape's wheel-well—'I do have my dress.'

I gave it a beat. 'And it is red and short and nigh unto dazzling.'

'I'm sure it'll be gorgeous on you.' Pavlik rose to his feet and pulled me up after him. 'Now, you go have fun and reserve tomorrow night.'

'For what?' We were standing toe-to-toe in the shadow of the liftgate.

'For us.' He gave me a proper kiss and went off to work.

WHEN I RE-ENTERED the Ristorante, clutching the bag containing my slut-dress and enough make-up to do it justice, the place seemed deserted. 'Helloooo?'

Getting no answer, I was about to leave when a workman stuck his head into the entry hall. 'Can I help you?'

'I was a guest at the show tonight. I'd like to use the bathroom?'

'Aren't you Maggy Thorsen?' he asked, eyes wide.

'Well, yes, but I—'

'Wow, great to meet you. I hear you took down the Realty Killer.'

Geez, Elaine Riordan already had a news slug. She'd like that distinction. Or not. The woman was crazy, so who could predict? 'But that was less than an hour ago. How did you recog—'

'This is the age of social networks,' he said, pulling out an iPhone. 'Look, you've already gone viral.'

Sure enough, there I was. Not a flattering shot, though. While I'm not a giant, I looked like a gorilla sitting on top of tiny, skinny Elaine Riordan. If I'd stood up, she could have been wedged in my butt crack like the poor Chihuahua in the fat-lady cartoon.

'Lovely,' I said. 'Though—'

'The press took off like a shot when word started to spread. The big man wasn't very happy about it, I have to say, but the media already had their story once the count was complete.'

'What did it come out to?'

'Only about fifty thousand.'

'Not a million?'

The man shrugged. 'Maybe the rest went sliding down the drain after the bag ripped. It's lucky any of it was salvaged, when you think about it. The plastic got hooked on a rough part, otherwise the whole thing would have been washed out to Jones Island.'

Milwaukee's sewage treatment plant. I thanked the man and asked again if it was OK for me to use the restroom.

'Sure, but I'm heading out and I think I'm the last of the crew. Here, take this.' He handed me a heavy brass key. 'I think I can trust you to lock up and stick it in the box that's hanging on the doorknob. I mean, after all, you're the star of the day.'

He held up his iPhone. 'Or at least the minute.'

Speaking of minutes, as I went into the bathroom I wondered how soon Eric would get wind of his mom's evening antics.

I didn't have to wait long. I had slipped into my dress and was finishing up my make-up when my smartphone vibrated on the marble counter next to the sink.

A text message. God forbid my only son would want to actually talk to me.

'What'd you do now, Mom?'

His punctuation, grammar and spelling had improved, now that we both had graduated to smartphones with real keyboards. Last year his message would have been: 'wut u do now, mm'.

I texted back. 'Captured a killer and saved humanity. More on News at Ten. Love you.'

I had time to run a brush through my hair before receiving, 'Love you, too. Night.'

I had barely set the phone down again before it began vibrating once more. This time a Twitter link, forwarded from Eric: 'Coffeehouse owner takes down serial killer'.

Probably with the same damn photo. I thought for a second and then texted to Eric. 'Hate the visual. Can you find a better pic of me and post it?'

Thirty seconds later: 'My high school graduation? I can cut myself out, if you want.'

Back from me: 'No! Leave you in!!' Love those exclamation points.

And, finally, a sign-off from Eric, more reminiscent of our old days of texting: 'LOL :-)'

He and I were living in an entirely different world than my parents' and mine. I balanced on one foot to slip on a red stiletto and fastened its strap around my ankle.

Eric had gotten his first cellphone when he was all of twelve, though admittedly just for emergency purposes. When I was twelve back in the seventies, there'd been no cellphones, no personal computers—at least so far as I knew.

My mother had been a self-proclaimed, technology-shunning hippie. In fact, one of my earliest memories was being taken by her, me at age four, to the first Earth Day, started by US Senator Gaylord Nelson of Wisconsin.

Now, I thought, putting my make-up back in the Pick

'n Save, recycling was a fact of life and 'paper or plastic' was an everyday…

I stopped. Cold.

'Holy shit,' I whispered into the mirror.

TWENTY-ONE

I DON'T RECOMMEND snooping around while wearing slut heels and a dress that slides nearly up to your waist when you lean forward enough to see the toes of said shoes.

In fact, I'm not sure I recommend snooping around, period, especially in a slaughterhouse.

I reached through the hidden doorway from the boardroom to switch on the light, just as Elaine Riordan had done earlier in the day when she showed Tien and me the room and its closet escape route.

Seemed like years ago now.

The fluorescent fixture buzzed, then flickered weakly, giving me just enough illumination to step through into the slaughterhouse. By the added light from a street lamp barely shining through a dirty window set high in the concrete block wall, I could see that—unlike in the Ristorante, where all of the equipment had been broken down—here the crew had left some items, including the flood lamps.

I picked my way across the disgustingly stained 'killing floor', praying that I wouldn't catch a heel or turn an ankle in a covered drain. Or, *much* worse, slide down an opened one, hem scrunched up to my armpits. I took three deep, if dank, breaths and found the plug for one of the flood lamps.

It would have made a whole lot more sense to change back into my other clothes, but my plan was to still attend the party at Sapphire. After, that is, a quick look for signs of tampering with the drain from which Ward Chitown had fished the money bag.

The candlepower of that one light allowed me to see that the slaughterhouse was pretty much as we'd left the place, including the drain cover, which sat to the right of its hole.

I tried to think things through. Probably made some sense for the crew to leave the awkward—and, unlike cameras, relatively inexpensive—pieces of gear on-site, especially if Chitown was hoping to field interview requests. The scene of the crime, and I do mean crime.

Because, of course, plastic grocery bags as we know them today just weren't available in 1974. More like the early eighties, when I was in high school and old enough to be embarrassed by my mother, who refused to accept them on environmental grounds.

A green pioneer, my mother, but that was beside the point.

The supposed loot from Romano's Raid could not have been hidden in the bag I saw resurrected from the drain hole. At least not in 1974.

I crouched down near the opening, tottering a bit. I was trying to see inside the drain itself to where the bag supposedly had snagged, but I was blocking my own light. Getting up, I tried the other side, but the pillar I'd nearly run into earlier that day cast its own shadow as well. I'd left the bag with my clothes and purse in the bathroom, but I'd brought my keychain, which had a tiny Maglight attached to it.

I flicked the switch.

Incredible how much light the thing threw, though I was having trouble steadying it enough to see anything. I gave in and gingerly touched the pillar with my fingertips for balance and tried again. About two feet down the hole was a protrusion, where the bag could have hung. Chitown had managed to snag the thing with a screwdriver to bring it up, but it would have been a lot tougher to hang it there originally. Especially since one slip might mean the loss of $50,000.

I got back up with an effort and looked around. 'The meat hooks,' I said, forcing myself to toddle over there. Most of them were too big to fit down the drain, but one...

'Looking for something?'

I turned to see Ward Chitown, who'd changed into a different designer suit and what looked like hand-made Italian loafers. 'Nope, just snooping. It's kind of my thing.'

'So I've heard.' He crossed to me. 'Quite the collection, don't you think?' His hand gesture toward the hooks was graceful, his voice as silky smooth as the leather of his shoes.

'Quite the coup, too.' I began backing away from the 'collection', not able to see where my own heels were landing. 'I mean, your find and all.'

Even I could hear the panic in my voice. I'd confronted a serial killer outside and taken her down. Now I was with a man I suspected of mere fraud, but my knees were shaking.

'Beautiful dress,' Chitown said. 'And you look lovely in it.'

'Thanks, but since we're probably late for the party, why don't I meet you over there.'

He caught my arm. 'I think we should talk here for a moment first.'

'Here?' The slaughterhouse, as before, was giving me incremental heebie-jeebies. I wanted to scream and run, but I'd have to take off the high heels first and they had ankle straps.

I doubted that Chitown would wait for me to squat down and undo them, even if I could make myself risk coming into significant personal contact with a floor that had absorbed the blood of countless animals. Even people.

And my hope was that yours truly would not be added to that last body count.

OK, I said to myself, enough mindless fear.

I took a deep breath. 'Listen, I think it was a really clever stunt, and believe me, no one will hear about it from me.'

'No?' The word came from behind the concrete pillar, Deirdre Doty rolling her shoulders around it and coming into sight wearing the same outfit she'd had on earlier, sans jacket. The lacy little cami showed, as well as her toned arms, which I didn't think I'd ever seen. Apparently, I hadn't heard her come in over the beating of my heart.

'Of course not,' I said, trying to iron out my voice. 'I spent a lot of years doing events and public relations. You pulled off the ultimate magic trick—nobody *really* wants to know how it was done.'

'You did.' The corners of Doty's mouth lifted a fraction, but that was the extent of anything you could call a smile. Or even a grin.

Under the dress, I was sweating like crazy and the rash on my hand was itching even worse. I couldn't resist scratching.

'Oh look, Ward. She's wringing her hands.' Doty's voice bizarrely reminded me of Barbara Billingsley, the actress who played the mother on the old TV show, *Leave it to Beaver*—probably because the father's character on the program was also named Ward. But Deirdre Doty was no June Cleaver.

'I wasn't wringing…' I started to say, then I caught a slightly different angle of light on her bare arm.

'What's that?' I gestured toward a red patch on her forearm that looked an awful lot like the one on my hand.

'Nothing.' She hid it behind her like a kid caught stealing candy.

I felt the balance of power shift, if not reverse itself, though nothing had really changed except my attitude. There was probably a lesson in that. 'It is *too* something. It's a rash, like mine from a trumpet creeper. How'd you get yours?'

'What do you mean?' Now Doty was backing away from me.

I chanced an advance. 'I got this when I touched the plant that was growing by the doorway of the so-called waiting room under the depot's loading dock the day we discovered Brigid's body. I could understand him—' I pointed to Chitown—'maybe touching it, but you weren't there then. You'd left to make some calls. At least, that's what you told us.'

Her eyes went wide. 'I…'

Chitown chimed in. 'We have to be honest with her, Deirdre.'

I pivoted, careful to keep both of them in view. 'So why don't you start, Ward? Tell me about the money you planted. There was no hidden loot—you made the whole thing up.'

'It was a stunt, as you said, but nothing more.' All of a sudden, Chitown looked like a broken man. 'The money was mine, Maggy.'

'You sacrificed your own money? You may not even get it back.'

'It's a fifty-thousand-dollar *investment*, one that could bring me another show of my own, especially if our production clips go viral on the Internet. I could even launch my own webcast, which, believe me, is the future of this medium we've been calling television.'

'You could have done that without spending a small fortune. Apparently even little me is all over the social networks.' I'd have shown him, but I'd had to leave my phone in my purse. No pockets in slut dresses.

'So I've heard.' Chitown didn't look happy.

'OK, I think I buy that you didn't mean any harm. But what about Brigid Ferndale?'

Doty said, 'We found her here.'

A hollow tone. 'When?' I asked.

'Monday night, when we came to scout the place.'

I thought I saw a chink in the armor of their new 'truth'. 'But Deirdre, Brigid didn't leave Sapphire until after you did. How could the two of you have found her?'

Doty blinked three times in rapid succession. 'I had to wait for Ward.'

Now Chitown was frowning at her oddly. 'No, Deirdre, that's not accurate. You called me when you left Sapphire and I was standing outside the Ristorante when you arrived.'

'What did you do then?' My question was directed at Chitown.

'Deirdre undid the lockbox and we took out the key to the restaurant's front door. We'd requested that the internal electricity be turned on, so we walked through the dining room, etc., deciding where to shoot what.'

'And from there into the slaughterhouse. Is that when you planted the money?'

'I did,' Doty said. An offhand wave at her boss. 'Ward was wearing a suit.'

'Do you always do his dirty work?'

She shrugged.

'Did you use a meat hook to lower the bag into the drain?'

She nodded, not looking at me.

'Whose idea was it to use a plastic bag?'

'Mine,' Doty said. 'That way the actual money would be protected and a small slit in the bottom would let people think the rest of the bills had been lost down the drain and into the sewer.'

'Good plan, but unfortunately plastic grocery bags weren't around in 1974.' I threw Chitown a glance. 'Next time you might want to conspire with someone who has a little more historical perspective. You know, like… Elaine Riordan? In fact, I'm surprised she didn't catch the "paper or plastic" problem herself. Or did she?'

'If she did,' Doty snapped, 'at least *she* knew enough to keep her mouth shut.'

'Of course she did,' I said. 'Elaine wanted not only to be *like* you, she wanted to *be* you.'

'And why not? I'm damn good at my job. I do everything for Ward and he, he...' Doty let it wither away.

'And he doesn't appreciate you, right? And to add insult to injury, you have to watch him charm other women. Is that the real reason Elaine didn't give you away? Because she's also crazy about Ward?'

Besides being just plain crazy.

I continued along the same tack. 'I bet there are a lot of women who fancy themselves in love with the big man. That must be hard for you. You even tried flirting with the sheriff. Tell me, did Ward even notice?'

'I don't flirt.' Doty had sunk into sullen now.

I changed it up. 'So, where did you find Brigid's body?'

Now, finally, Chitown spoke up. 'Deirdre saw her after placing the money. The...corpse was hidden behind that pillar.'

'*That* pillar?' I pointed, remembering the stain I imagined was wet when I touched it. 'Did Brigid hit her head, Deirdre?'

She shook her head, lips tight.

'No, no,' Chitown said. 'You have it all wrong, Maggy. The young woman was *already* dead. We just moved the body.' He actually seemed ashamed. 'I'm not proud of it, but your Brigid simply couldn't be found here. It would have ruined our whole plan.'

'How did you know about the room under the depot?'

Doty fielded that one, if grudgingly. 'Elaine told me about the waiting area, along with a million other "fascinating" factoids, when I met with her at the Historical Society. Honest to God, you couldn't shut the woman up.'

Including the morning we'd found Brigid Ferndale's body. No wonder Riordan had been so open about the room's existence. She'd had no idea what awaited us inside. 'Were you trying to frame Elaine? Did you know she'd killed the other women?'

'Of course not,' Doty said. 'How could we? I just figured she was another whack job infatuated with Ward.'

Who the bigger 'whack job' was, remained to be seen. 'So, you put Brigid's body under the depot. And, if there hadn't been a ventilation shaft allowing the stench of decomposition to waft up and we'd never gone to investigate, no one would have been the wiser.' I paused. 'Not even Brigid's family.'

Doty just shook her head again, but Chitown replied to me, 'Deirdre and I were well aware of the killings, if not the identity of the killer. When we found the body, we just knew your Brigid had to be another victim killed showing a property.'

'My' Brigid, again. Like a parent who, when the kids misbehaved, disclaimed ownership: 'Look at what *your* son did'. Though in this case, 'my Brigid'—party girl, social climber, someone's daughter—had simply died. And done so at the hands of somebody within ten feet of me. And I wasn't going to let that pass.

'But Brigid wasn't "another victim",' I said. 'Ward, you're not thinking clearly. First of all, Brigid died from blunt trauma to the head. The other women were shot through the head. Second, witnesses say that Brigid left Sapphire a good twenty minutes after

Deirdre, who supposedly came directly here. There's
only one conclusion.'

Make them wait for it. 'One or both of you killed
Brigid Ferndale.'

TWENTY-TWO

WARD CHITOWN NEEDED only two strides to reach Deirdre Doty and shake her by the shoulders. 'My God, Deirdre. Is Maggy right? Did you actually kill the Ferndale girl? Oh, you've ruined everything for me.'

Oh, boy. And I'd thought Elaine Riordan was a sociopath.

Doty held up both her hands, now trying to back away. 'I did not. *She* was going to ruin it, Ward. That nosy, greedy bitch caught me hiding your money. Said she'd tell everybody unless we cut her in.'

'I could have handled that,' Chitown said, giving Doty another shake, but his heart didn't seem to be in it. 'Why didn't you at least let me talk to her?'

'I think I can answer that,' I said to Chitown. 'You never actually met her, Ward. In fact, the only reason you knew the "real estate agent for the Ristorante" was a lovely young blonde, as you put it last night, was that you had seen her dead. Here.'

I waited for a denial from either quarter but, getting none, pushed on. 'Deirdre, though, *did* meet Brigid and it didn't take thirty minutes to realize that the young woman was not only beautiful, but ambitious and utterly ruthless. Women like Kate McNamara and Elaine Riordan were always buzzing around you, but Brigid was different. Deirdre didn't want her anywhere near you, much less as a partner.'

Deirdre Doty moved both hands to Chitown's chest now, pleading. 'She was a user, Ward. Yes, a star-fucker, like all the rest, except this one was smart. That bitch would have chewed even you up and spat you out.' Doty dropped her chin to her chest. 'She called you a…has-been.'

Chitown released her, then started to pace. Nervously now, unlike the measured showman on stage earlier that day. 'Oh, God, Deirdre. What have you done?'

'I did it for you,' she said, trying to fall into step with him.

'Did you push her, Deirdre?' I asked. 'Or maybe it was an accident? Brigid stumbled and hit her head.'

'That was it.' Now the poor producer was nodding like crazy, words suddenly tumbling out at a frantic pace. 'We argued and I… When she called you a has-been, Ward, I couldn't stand it and I pushed her. Brigid fell back and hit her head on the pillar there.'

Doty pointed and I wiped my hand on my dress, futilely hoping to forget the stickiness.

'You're going to jail,' Chitown shouted. 'Do you understand that, you little twit?'

The producer looked like she'd been clouted. Her mouth opened and closed like a dying goldfish before she finally turned to me. 'Ward helped me with all of it, Maggy. Cleaning up the blood and loading the body into her car. We backed up to the depot's loading dock and I took the flashlight and found the door and opened it. Ward helped me carry her into the bathroom, too. Then we left her car in your parking lot, after I wiped off all the places I thought we could have left fingerprints.'

Ward Chitown seemed stunned, as though he could never have imagined his producer would withdraw loyalty from him the way he just had from her.

'Sounds like accessory-after-the-fact,' I said, remembering the rut I'd noticed next to the sidewalk leading to the passenger platform stairs. One tire on the concrete and one on the grass.

'You little bitch,' Chitown now screamed, coming at her. 'I'll, I'll…testify against you.'

Doty backed up and, finding herself against the wall of meat hooks, grabbed one. 'Stay away from me, Ward, or I'll finish things here.'

Uh-oh. I may have set all this in motion, but it was getting out of hand and I didn't know what to do.

Where was the cavalry when you needed them?

Chitown either didn't hear Deirdre or didn't care. Like Pavlik had said about people who'd been foreclosed on and pushed into bankruptcy. When you've lost everything, you have nothing left to lose.

Neither of these people felt they had anything to lose. Which was a very bad thing for me. I turned to run, my heels making clickety-clacks on the concrete floor like a long-legged tap-dancer. Sprint-wise, though, a rather slow one.

From way too close behind me, Doty screamed. 'Ward, we can't let her go!'

Before I turned around, Doty must have broken free from a lagging, seemingly indecisive Chitown. And she was coming at me, meat hook raised high in her right hand, the rusty 'business' point of it about two feet above my eye-level.

I thought, Eric, I'm so sorry.

Then Doty was swinging the hook in a vicious arc toward my face.

Thankfully, my *second* thought was, Pavlik taught me what to do.

I ducked to the left and Doty's follow-through sent her lunging, like a tennis player whose attempt at serving resulted in her racket missing the ball completely.

As Doty caught her balance, I cocked the heel of my right hand at the wrist and, before she could raise the hook again, I drove that heel up and into her nose.

And immediately realized that Pavlik had emphasized doing something *else* before heel-of-hand-to-nose.

I clamped my eyes closed. 'Oh, shit, shit, *SHIT*!'

But, as soon as my lids flapped back open, there was Deirdre Doty, writhing at my feet, meat hook a leg-length away. Both her hands were held to her nose, trying unsuccessfully to staunch the blood.

Cool.

With adrenaline pumping so hard I was afraid my eardrums would blow out, I rasped—insanely, I might add—'Hey, Ward, you want a shot at me, too?'

Apparently he did indeed.

Since trying to run in these heels had proved futile, I stood my ground as Chitown easily closed the distance between us and grabbed me by the throat with both hands.

This time, though, I remembered *exactly* what Pavlik taught me.

I lifted my right knee about a foot, and Chitown dropped his left hand to his groin area, probably figuring I was going to knee him you-know-where.

Instead, using his own chokehold as support, I stomped my four-inch stiletto heel as hard as I could into and, hopefully, through, his supple Italian leather shoe.

CHITOWN WAS STILL hopping on one foot as I bolted through the closet and straight into the man who'd taught me lifesaving. Literally.

'You got my text message?' I asked, noting the gun in his hand.

'I did,' he said, signaling the deputies behind him to continue on into the slaughterhouse. 'But apparently you didn't get mine, asking you to wait until we arrived before you went nosing around.'

'Sorry,' I said sheepishly, running my palms down my dress as if to straighten out any wrinkles. 'No place for a cellphone.'

I NEVER DID make it to Sapphire that night.

Pavlik arrived at my place around 2 a.m. I'd waited up.

'Everything taken care of?' I asked as I poured wine into his glass and settled onto the couch next to him. Frank had fallen asleep on the floor in front of us, his big furry head using one of Pavlik's feet as a crude pillow.

'Ward Chitown and Deirdre Doty are both talking, nonstop though separately. Accusations against the other of everything including federal tax fraud. And apparently the apple doesn't fall far from the tree. You know that $50,000 they planted in the drain?'

'Yes,' I said, snuggling under his arm.

'It really was the loot.'

That jolted me. 'You mean from 1974? But how could that be? Where did Chitown find it?'

'His father's safe. Apparently the old man was a bent cop—or, in his case, FBI agent. Chitown Senior must have found the cash during the raid and squirreled it until he could return to the scene and retrieve it.'

'The whole *million*?'

'If that much was there. All Chitown Junior says he found in that safe was the fifty grand. He figured he'd use it to prime the pump on his new career.'

'Career. What a—'

'Hey, speaking of careers,' Pavlik continued. 'I hear you're an online sensation.'

'I look like a walrus birthing a baby seal.'

'Perhaps, but you're a gorgeous walrus.' He tipped my chin up and kissed my lips.

'Did you notice my red dress?'

'Hard to miss it. It was rolled up around your waist when you burst through that closet back in the restaurant.'

Aww, geez. Good thing that photo op wasn't going viral.

Pavlik lowered his voice to a lion's purr. 'But maybe you'll wear it for me another time?'

'It would be my pleasure.' I began playing with the fine hairs at the nape of his head.

Pavlik's eyes were closed and he gave a little moan. 'Mmmm. And maybe take it off for me another time, too?'

'Nope.'

His eyes flew open. 'Why not?'

'That's your job.'

* * * * *

REQUEST YOUR FREE BOOKS!
2 FREE NOVELS PLUS 2 FREE GIFTS!

⊕ HARLEQUIN®

INTRIGUE

BREATHTAKING ROMANTIC SUSPENSE

HII5

REQUEST YOUR FREE BOOKS!

2 FREE NOVELS PLUS 2 FREE GIFTS!

ROMANTIC suspense

Sparked by danger, fueled by passion

YES! Please send me 2 FREE Harlequin® Romantic Suspense novels and my 2 FREE gifts (gifts are worth about $10). After receiving them, if I don't wish to receive any more books, I can return the shipping statement marked "cancel." If I don't cancel, I will receive 4 brand-new novels every month and be billed just $4.74 per book in the U.S. or $5.49 per book in Canada. That's a savings of at least 12% off the cover price! It's quite a bargain! Shipping and handling is just 50¢ per book in the U.S. and 75¢ per book in Canada.* I understand that accepting the 2 free books and gifts places me under no obligation to buy anything. I can always return a shipment and cancel at any time. Even if I never buy another book, the two free books and gifts are mine to keep forever.

240/340 HDN GH3P

Name	(PLEASE PRINT)

Address		Apt. #

City	State/Prov.	Zip/Postal Code

Signature (if under 18, a parent or guardian must sign)

Mail to the **Reader Service:**

IN U.S.A.: P.O. Box 1867, Buffalo, NY 14240-1867
IN CANADA: P.O. Box 609, Fort Erie, Ontario L2A 5X3

Want to try two free books from another line?
Call 1-800-873-8635 or visit www.ReaderService.com.

* Terms and prices subject to change without notice. Prices do not include applicable taxes. Sales tax applicable in N.Y. Canadian residents will be charged applicable taxes. Offer not valid in Quebec. This offer is limited to one order per household. Not valid for current subscribers to Harlequin Romantic Suspense books. All orders subject to credit approval. Credit or debit balances in a customer's account(s) may be offset by any other outstanding balance owed by or to the customer. Please allow 4 to 6 weeks for delivery. Offer available while quantities last.

Your Privacy—The Reader Service is committed to protecting your privacy. Our Privacy Policy is available online at www.ReaderService.com or upon request from the Reader Service.

We make a portion of our mailing list available to reputable third parties that offer products we believe may interest you. If you prefer that we not exchange your name with third parties, or if you wish to clarify or modify your communication preferences, please visit us at www.ReaderService.com/consumerschoice or write to us at Reader Service Preference Service, P.O. Box 9062, Buffalo, NY 14240-9062. Include your complete name and address.

REQUEST YOUR FREE BOOKS!

2 FREE NOVELS
FROM THE SUSPENSE COLLECTION
PLUS 2 FREE GIFTS!

YES! Please send me 2 FREE novels from the Suspense Collection and my 2 FREE gifts (gifts are worth about $10). After receiving them, if I don't wish to receive any more books, I can return the shipping statement marked "cancel." If I don't cancel, I will receive 4 brand-new novels every month and be billed just $6.49 per book in the U.S. or $6.99 per book in Canada. That's a savings of at least 19% off the cover price. It's quite a bargain! Shipping and handling is just 50¢ per book in the U.S. and 75¢ per book in Canada.* I understand that accepting the 2 free books and gifts places me under no obligation to buy anything. I can always return a shipment and cancel at any time. Even if I never buy another book, the two free books and gifts are mine to keep forever.

191/391 MDN GH4Z

Name _____ (PLEASE PRINT) _____

Address _____ Apt. # _____

City _____ State/Prov. _____ Zip/Postal Code _____

Signature (if under 18, a parent or guardian must sign)

Mail to the **Reader Service:**
IN U.S.A.: P.O. Box 1867, Buffalo, NY 14240-1867
IN CANADA: P.O. Box 609, Fort Erie, Ontario L2A 5X3

Want to try two free books from another line?
Call 1-800-873-8635 or visit www.ReaderService.com.

* Terms and prices subject to change without notice. Prices do not include applicable taxes. Sales tax applicable in N.Y. Canadian residents will be charged applicable taxes. Offer not valid in Quebec. This offer is limited to one order per household. Not valid for current subscribers to the Suspense Collection or the Romance/Suspense Collection. All orders subject to credit approval. Credit or debit balances in a customer's account(s) may be offset by any other outstanding balance owed by or to the customer. Please allow 4 to 6 weeks for delivery. Offer available while quantities last.

Your Privacy—The Reader Service is committed to protecting your privacy. Our Privacy Policy is available online at www.ReaderService.com or upon request from the Reader Service.

We make a portion of our mailing list available to reputable third parties that offer products we believe may interest you. If you prefer that we not exchange your name with third parties, or if you wish to clarify or modify your communication preferences, please visit us at www.ReaderService.com/consumerschoice or write to us at Reader Service Preference Service, P.O. Box 9062, Buffalo, NY 14240-9062. Include your complete name and address.

SUS15

READERSERVICE.COM

Manage your account online!

- Review your order history
- Manage your payments
- Update your address

*We've designed the
Reader Service website
just for you.*

Enjoy all the features!

- Discover new series available to you, and read excerpts from any series.
- Respond to mailings and special monthly offers.
- Connect with favorite authors at the blog.
- Browse the Bonus Bucks catalog and online-only exculsives.
- Share your feedback.

Visit us at:

ReaderService.com

RS15